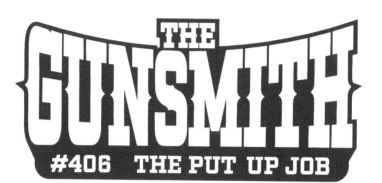

THE GUNSMITH

#406 THE PUT UP JOB

THE GUNSMITH #406: THE PUT UP JOB
A Pro Se Press Publication

THE PUT UP JOB is a work of historical fiction. Many of the important historical events, figures, and locations are as accurately portrayed as possible. In keeping with a work of fiction, various events and occurrences were invented by the author.

Edited by Tommy Hancock
Editor in Chief, Pro Se Productions—Tommy Hancock
Submissions Editor—Rachel Lampi
Director of Corporate Operations—Kristi King-Morgan
Publisher & Pro Se Productions, LLC-Chief Executive Officer—Fuller Bumpers

Cover Art by Jeffrey Hayes
Print Production and Book Design by Percival Constantine
New Pulp Logo Design by Sean E. Ali
New Pulp Seal Design by Cari Reese

Pro Se Productions, LLC
133 1/2 Broad Street
Batesville, AR, 72501
870-834-4022

editorinchief@prose-press.com
www.prose-press.com

THE GUNSMITH #406: THE PUT UP JOB

Published in digital form by Piccadilly Publishing,

THE GUNSMITH

#406 THE PUT UP JOB

J.R. ROBERTS

PRO SE PRESS

ONE

Clint had only been in Festus, Wyoming a few hours when he got his first taste of what rancher Vance Restin was really like.

He had just come out of the Six of Spades Saloon after washing his lunch down with a cold beer. Festus was a mid-sized town that was on its way up, with new buildings popping up on almost every street. From the talk he overheard in the saloon while leaning over his beer, everybody seemed pretty excited about the town's growth.

Just outside the batwing doors he was stretching and taking a breath when he noticed some commotion across the street.

Two men seemed to have gotten to the door of the general store at the same time, one going in—a bigger, more well-dressed man--and the other coming out, and bumped into each other. The man going in seemed to take great exception to the incident, and Clint could hear his booming voice from across the street.

"Why the hell don't you get out of the way, man?" he demanded. "Don't you see me here?"

The other man spoke more softly. Clint couldn't hear the words, but he had the impression he was apologizing.

"Never mind that, just get out of my way!"

The man stepped aside, and as he did a small boy

started out the door. Again, the larger man became impatient and actually pushed the lad aside. The boy stumbled, but his father caught him before he could tumble from the boardwalk.

As the larger man entered, a woman came out the door, stumbling as if she had also been pushed. Clint assumed the arrogant man had done so. Effectively, he had shoved the entire family out of his way rather than wait for them to exit the store first. Clint hated men who felt they were entitled that way, that people should step aside whenever they saw them.

He knew he shouldn't, but he stepped into the street and crossed over.

"You folks okay?" he asked.

The little family turned to face him, and the father said, "Yes, sir. We're fine. That was just Mr. Restin."

"Restin?"

"He's a bad man," the boy said.

"He's a horrible, horrible man," the woman said. "He thinks people should get out of his way right quick whenever they see him."

"And why would he think that?" Clint asked.

"Easy," the woman said. "He has the biggest ranch in the county and thinks he owns everything in town--and his men are all over the place." She glared across the street.

Clint turned to look in the direction of her glare, saw four men standing in front of the hardware store. He'd seen some men inside the saloon who looked like ranch hands as well. These four were lounging insolently, wearing guns and making comments to any woman who walked by.

"They're as ill-mannered as their boss," she said, her pretty face showing her distaste.

"Now, Jennifer—"

"Never mind!" she snapped at her husband. "We got a right to speak up. This man's a stranger, and he asked."

The boy was looking through the door at the inside of the store and he said, "We better get outta the way, he's comin' out."

"Is that so?" Clint asked.

"Yeah," the boy said. "Better move, Mister, or he'll knock you down."

Clint grinned at the boy and said, "Let's see..."

"Mister—" the man said.

"Leave him alone, Ben," the woman said. "I want to see this."

Clint could see through the door that the man they called Restin was heading his way. He deliberately stepped into the doorway so they'd get there at the same time.

As Restin came face-to-face with Clint—standing several inches taller, and some twenty or thirty pounds heavier—he glared. He was also about ten years older.

"Stand aside!" he barked.

"I'm going inside," Clint said.

"Well, stand aside," the rancher said again. "You can go in after I've left."

"I think you should stand aside and let me in," Clint said. "Show some consideration to a stranger in your town."

The man's face turned red as his anger grew.

"Now look, friend," he said, "I don't stand aside for anyone, especially not some saddle tramp driftin' through town. Now I'll say it again. Move aside."

"Nope," Clint said. "You move."

"You're askin' for it!"

"I'm just asking to go inside," Clint said.

"My men are right across the street—"

"Well, you can wave at them after I go inside," Clint said. "Here, let me help you move aside."

Clint grabbed the front of the man's jacket, yanked him out of the store, spun him around, and shoved him. He'd only meant to push him aside, but Restin's right foot went back and stepped off the boardwalk, and the man went tumbling to the dirt, kicking up a cloud.

"Uh-oh," Ben said.

The four men across the street started forward...

TWO

"Here," Clint said, to Restin, "let me give you a hand. I didn't mean to dump you in the street."

The man glared at Clint and slapped his outstretched hand aside.

"You'll pay for this!" he snapped.

Clint withdrew his hand and stepped back as the four men reached their employer.

"Hey boss," one of them said as two others reached down and helped him to his feet, "what's goin' on here?"

"You got trouble?" one asked.

"I don't have trouble," Restin said. "This fella here has the trouble."

One of the men looked at Clint and said, "That right, Mister? You want trouble?"

Clint studied the four men more closely and realized he'd misread them the first time. They were not ranch hands—they were hired guns. He knew it from the way they stood and the way they wore their guns.

"Kill this man!" Restin said to his men.

"Really?" Beth said, stepping forward.

"Beth—" her husband said.

But his wife continued. "Because he pushed you out of the way you're gonna have four of your gunmen kill him? Because he hurt your ego? You're a crazy man, Mr. Restin."

The rancher looked at her, then at her husband.

"You should control your wife, Ben," he said. "Get her out of the way."

"It's all right, Ma'am," Clint said, putting his hand on the woman's arm. "I can handle this."

"No, it's not okay," she said. "I know you done what you did because of us—"

"It's okay," Clint assured her. "Just go over there and stand with your boy."

"Mama?" the boy said.

"It's all right, Harry," she said, stepping over to him and putting her hands on his shoulders. "It's all right." She glared at her husband, who was apparently useless for anything beyond carrying packages—which he was.

Clint turned to Restin and his four men.

"Restin, these men pull their guns, a lot of innocent people are going to get hurt," he said, "but I promise you one thing."

"What's that?"

"You'll be dead.' Clint said. "And I'll kill you first."

One of the four men moved up alongside another and whispered something to him.

"Are you sure?" the man asked. He was the one who asked Clint about trouble.

The first man nodded.

The other man stepped up next to his boss and said something into his ear.

"What? Are you sure?" Restin asked.

His man nodded.

Restin looked at Clint.

"Look," the rancher said, "it was just a misunderstanding. Let's forget it."

"Why don't you apologize to these nice people?" Clint asked. "Then we'll forget it."

People had gathered around to witness the confrontation.

Restin looked over at the family of three. The man appeared concerned, the boy excited, and the woman, Beth, angry. She held the boy close to her.

"I'm sorry, Ben," Restin said. "Mrs. Ballard. My apologies."

"And the boy," Clint said.

"Young man," Restin said, tightly, "you have my apologies."

"You're a bad man!" the boy said.

"So I've been told," Restin said. He turned to his men and yelled, "Come on!"

He stormed away, the four men following him. The one Clint now knew had recognized him kept looking over his shoulder, to make sure Clint wouldn't shoot him in the back.

Everyone remained silent until Restin and his men were gone.

"That was great!" Beth exclaimed.

"What happened, there?" Ben asked. "Why did he do that?"

At that moment somebody started yelling, "Clear the streets!"

Clint turned and looked, saw a man with a badge break through the crowd.

"Come on," he shouted, "move it along."

As the crowd began to disperse the lawman turned and looked at Clint.

"Adams, you're coming with me."

"What for?" Beth asked. "He didn't do anything."

"Mrs. Ballard," the sheriff said, "just...mind your own business."

"This is my business!" she said. She turned to Clint.

7

"Come to our house for supper tonight. After he finishes with you."

"Mrs. Ballard—"

Ben Ballard said, "She won't take no for an answer."

"Just follow Harry," she said. "He'll bring you."

"Adams!" the sheriff snapped. "Come with me."

"All right!" Clint said, to all of them.

THREE

"**W**hat the hell, Adams?" the sheriff asked, sitting behind his desk. "When you got here and came to me, you promised you wouldn't look for trouble. Now I find you takin' on the biggest man in the county."

"He was taking me on," Clint said. "He sent his four hired guns after me."

"How the hell did you avoid gunplay?"

"One of them recognized me."

"Ah. And what's this about you and the Ballard family? What's that about?"

"Nothing," Clint said. "We just met in front of the general store. Who are they?"

"A family," Sheriff Moreland said, "just a family. Ben works in town, Beth makes dresses and sells them in the general store."

"And what's the story with this fellow Restin?"

"The same story as anybody with money," the lawman said. "His success went to his head. Now he treats people like shit and keeps hired guns around to make sure he stays alive."

"How involved is he with the town?"

"Whataya mean, like politics?"

"Like anything," Clint said. "Somebody said he thinks he owns the town."

"Well, he owns a few businesses, and he sits on the

town council. But he ain't runnin' for Mayor that I know of."

"I see."

"You gotta stay out of his way, Adams," Moreland said. "I don't want you to end up killin' any of his men or, God forbid, him. Get it?"

"I get it, Sheriff."

"Now, you were tellin' me the truth, right?" the lawman asked. "You were just passin' through?"

"On my way from nowhere to nowhere," Clint said. "Your town just looked sort of interesting."

"Well, do us all a favor," Moreland said. "Satisfy your interest and move on, huh?"

"Don't worry, Sheriff," Clint said. "I won't be staying much longer."

"Glad to hear it."

"Can I go now?"

"Yeah," Moreland said, with a wave, "go."

Clint stepped outside, found the boy, Harry, waiting for him there.

"What are you doing here, son?"

"I—I'm supposed to show you the way to our house," the boy said. "Ma said you was comin' ta supper."

"She did, huh?"

The boy nodded.

"Well, lead the way—Harry."

"Y-yes, sir."

*****

As they walked through town Clint said, "Harry, I hope your Mom is a good cook."

"She's a great cook, sir."

"That's good," Clint said. "What about you?"

10

"Sir?"

"You can stop calling me sir, Harry," Clint said. "Just call me Clint."

"All right, Clint."

"What do you do?"

"Me, si—Clint? I'm just a kid."

"Do you go to school?"

"Sure, I do."

"That's good. And what's your dad do?"

"He works around town."

"Doing what?"

"Anything he can, si—Clint. My dad knows how to do a lot of things."

"So he's good with his hands, huh?"

"He's real good. He can fix anything, or build any-thing," the boy said.

"You sound real proud of him."

"I am."

Clint had a feeling the man's wife didn't feel the same way the boy did.

They walked through town until they came to an area peppered with small houses. Harry led Clint to one of them, which, unlike the others, was not in a state of disrepair. If Ben Ballard was good at fixing things, it showed in the condition of his small home. The fence was perfect, and the house looked freshly painted.

"This is it," Harry said, waving his hand. "This is our house."

"It looks good, Harry," Clint said. "It looks real good." Clint took a deep breath. "And something else smells mighty good."

"That's my mom's pot roast," Harry said, taking a deep breath. "And it smells ready!

FOUR

Clint followed Harry into the house, which was very warm from the heat of the cast iron stove. On top of the stove were several steaming pots and pans.

"Mr. Adams," Ben Ballard said. He rose from the chair he was sitting in and approached Clint with his hand out. "Welcome to our home."

Clint shook his head. "Thanks for having me."

Beth Ballard turned from the stove, wiped her hands on an apron she wore around her waist. Clint hadn't noticed until now that her hair was the color of honey. It was mostly pinned up—mostly, because several tendrils had come loose and were hanging down around her face.

"Yes, welcome," she said, smiling. "I hope you brought your appetite."

"Oh yeah," Clint said. "Harry's been telling me what a great cook you are. I'm starving."

"Good, then you go and wash up, Harry. Supper's about ready to be put on the table."

"Have a seat, Clint," Ben said. "Can I get you a drink?"

"I'll just have some water with supper, thanks," Clint said, sitting at the table.

"I have some coffee made," Beth said.

"Then that would be even better."

He sat at the table and Beth brought him a cup of

coffee. Ben sat across from him, and Harry came running into the room and sat on his right.

Beth set several pots and bowls down on the table and then sat on his left.

"Dig in," she said. "Help yourself."

"I'll wait 'til Harry has his," Clint said.

Beth dished out meat and vegetables into Harry's plate, passing each bowl and pot to Clint after each. When they all had food on their plates they started eating.

"Did the sheriff give you a hard time?" Beth asked.

"He tried," Clint said. "Seems I promised him I'd stay out of trouble when I first came to town."

"Why would you have to do that?" Harry asked.

"Well, Harry," Clint said, "some people are just followed around by trouble."

"And you're one of those people?"

"Sometimes."

"I'm sorry," Beth said, "but we don't even know your name."

"His name is Clint," Harry said. "He said I can call him Clint."

"Clint?" Beth said.

"That's right."

"Those gunmen," Ben said, "they backed off. It was as if they...recognized you. And the way you made Restin apologize..."

"My name is Clint Adams."

Beth and Ben looked at each other across the table. Clint knew they recognized the name.

"Then that explains it," Ben said. "They were afraid of you."

"Why were they afraid of Clint?" Harry asked.

"Just eat your supper, Harry," Beth said. "Let the grown-ups talk."

"Aw, you always say that," he complained, but continued to eat.

They all ate for a few minutes in silence before Beth spoke again.

"W-why would a man like you—why did you help us?" she asked.

"I don't like seeing people pushed around," he said. "And I don't like people like Restin, who think they're entitled to treat people any way they want."

"He hasn't always been like that," Ben said. "We used to be..." he trailed off.

"What?" Clint asked, urging him to go on. "You used to be what?"

"Ben is under the impression that he and Vance Restin used to be friends."

"Is that right?" Clint looked at Ben.

"It was a long time ago," Ben said. "Before he got so..."

"Rich?"

"Yes."

"How long ago was that?"

"About eight years," Ben said.

"And he's gotten worse ever since," Beth said.

"Beth—" Ben started.

"You can't defend him anymore, Ben!" she snapped. "Look at how he treated you today. Like a perfect stranger."

"Beth..." Ben said again, but she wasn't listening.

"How is the pot roast?" she asked, turning to look at Clint.

"It's great," he said. "I haven't had a home cooked meal in a long time. This is...wonderful."

"I told you!" Harry said, proudly.

"Yes, you did."

"Take some more," Beth said.

"I think I will."

She passed him the platter with the meat on it, and there was no more talk of Vance Restin for the rest of the meal.

FIVE

While Beth cleared the table she told the men to go out front and wait for coffee. And she told Harry to go to his room and finish his homework.

Outside Ben offered Clint a cigar, and he accepted. The only time he ever smoked was when someone offered him one.

There were no chairs out there so they sat on the front step.

"Beth doesn't like Vance Restin very much, does she?" Clint asked.

"Not many people do."

"But you do," Clint said. "Or, you did."

"Once," Ben said, "a long time ago."

"What happened?"

Ben shrugged.

"We were friends and partners, and then we weren't," Ben said. "Beth would tell you he cheated me."

"You don't think so?"

"I think Vance did what he thought he had to do to succeed," Ben said.

"And you don't hold that against him?"

Ben shrugged.

"Who among us would not take that opportunity if it came?" Ben said.

"I know a few people who wouldn't turn on their

17

friends for money," Clint said.

"Then you're lucky," Ben said. "I don't know anybody like that."

"That's what's wrong with this town," Beth said. She was carrying two cups of coffee and handed them each one. "Nobody cares to do the right thing."

"The town seems to be growing," Clint said.

"Oh yes," she said, "we're getting nice new buildings. What we need now are some new people. And we need to get rid of Vance Restin and his gunmen."

"Does he have any family?" Clint asked.

"He has a wife and a daughter."

"What are they like?"

"His wife is...nice," Ben said.

"Maybe," Beth said, "but that daughter, she's a spoiled rotten bitch." She turned and went back inside.

"Is she right?" Clint asked. "About the daughter, I mean."

"Yeah, I'm afraid so," Ben said. "He wants to send her to California to be educated, but she doesn't want to go."

"Exactly how old a kid are we talking about, here?" Clint asked.

"No kid," Ben said. "She's probably...twenty."

"A lot of girls in the West are married by then," Clint said, "with children."

"He doesn't want that for her," Ben said.

"What does he want?"

Ben shrugged. "Something better."

"Don't you want that for Harry?"

"Of course."

"Then I guess the two of you have something in common."

"I guess so," Ben said. "Beth would hate to hear

18

that."

"She seems...angry," Clint said.

"She's always angry at me," Ben said. "She'd leave me, if she had any place to go. Not that I blame her."

"Why?" Clint asked. "Why don't you blame her?"

"I don't think we've loved each other for a while now," Ben said. "We're probably just staying together because of Harry."

"That's a shame," Clint said. "I'd probably stay with a woman like that for her cooking."

Ben grinned and they clinked coffee cups.

*****

When Clint left, thanking Beth for the delicious dinner, she walked him outside.

"Harry wanted to say goodbye," she told him, "but I made him go to bed."

"That's all right," Clint said. "I'll see him again before I leave."

She put her hand on his arm and said, "You're leaving? When?"

"I'm not sure," he said, "but soon."

"I hope I get to see you again before you leave town," she said.

He was uncomfortable with her hand on his arm, hoping that Ben wasn't watching from a window.

"I'm sure I'll see all of you before I go," Clint said.

He started to walk away but she tightened her grip on his forearm.

"I—I just want to thank You again for what you did for us," she said. "It was clear that Ben wasn't going to do anything."

"I'm sure Ben has his reasons for whatever he does."

"Or what he doesn't do, you mean," she said. "I don't know if you noticed, but my husband isn't the strongest man in the world."

"You never know how strong a man really is, Beth," he said, moving away from her touch. "Thanks again for supper."

He hurried away before she could say anything else.

SIX

Clint went directly to his hotel, where the desk clerk waved frantically at him as he walked through the lobby.

"This message came in for you, Mr. Adams," the man said.

"Who brought it?" Clint asked, accepting the piece of paper.

"Don't know," the man said, "just some fella. Looked like a ranch hand."

"Okay, thanks."

Clint took the message with him to his room and read it there. He was surprised to see that it was from Vance Restin. It was a note of apology and an invitation for Clint to come out to Restin's ranch the next day. He refolded the message and set it aside, not sure what he was going to do.

After his supper with the Ballard family, he wasn't feeling too kindly toward Vance Restin, but he had to admit that he was curious about the man. Ben Ballard seemed to have a hard time disliking the man, despite the way he'd been treated.

He had just removed his boots when there was a knock on the door. Removing his gun from the holster hanging on the bedpost he walked to the door.

"Who is it?" he asked.

"It's me," a woman's voice said, "Beth. Beth Ballard?"

Clint opened his door, keeping the gun behind his back.

"Beth, what are you doing—"

"Can I come in?"

"I don't kno—"

"Before someone sees me?" She seemed very nervous.

"Yes, all right," he said, "come in." She slid by him and he peered outside to check the hall before closing the door.

"What's going on, Beth?"

"Y-you said you were leaving town soon."

"Pretty soon, yeah," he said.

"Well, that doesn't give us much time, then."

"Time?" he asked. "Time for what?"

"For this."

She reached behind her, undid her simple cotton dress and let it fall to the floor.

"Beth—"

"Please," she said, "d-don't humiliate me by rejecting me." She lowered her eyes, then lifted them and looked into his. "Don't you like me?"

She had a lovely body, pale, slender, with breasts like ripe peaches. Her nipples were pink, with wide aureole, and she smelled like she was ready for anything but rejection.

"Beth, of course I like you," he said. "You're lovely, but—"

"Are you worried about Ben?"

"I usually stay away from married women," he said, "especially if I know the husband."

"You talked with my husband, Clint," she said. "I

know he told you about us. We don't have a marriage anymore. We're only staying together for Harry's sake." She crossed her arms in front of her. "I haven't been touched by a man in months."

"Beth—"She took a few steps closer to him and dropped her hands.

"When you came across that street to help us, my heart started to race," she told him. "When you dumped Vance Restin into the street I could hardly breathe. The whole time you were having supper with my family I wanted to jump across the table at you." She moved closer. "Don't tell me a woman has never come to your room and offered herself to you."

"No, it's not that," he said. "Yes, it's happened, but no—"

"So do you think you're gonna get out of this room without this happening?" she asked.

It had happened to him before—many times, in fact. Women were attracted to a man with a gun. It happened. And except for the ones who really came to his room to kill him—or to help somebody kill him—no, he had not gotten out of the room without it happening.

And to tell the truth, when there was a naked woman in his room, like this—a lovely, vibrant, naked woman who smelled the way Beth Ballard smelled now, he wanted it to happen.

Actually, hours later he thought about the way Beth smelled in his room. Every woman had their own aroma when they were aroused. He'd never encountered one that wasn't pleasant and didn't arouse him as well. Some were more arousing than others.

The odor of Beth Ballard's arousal was particularly strong. He wondered if it had anything to do with the fact that she hadn't been excited—or quite this excited—in many months.

At the moment, though, he gave himself up to the naked woman in his room. Why not? There would be time enough later to think about everything else.

He reached for her, grabbed her by the hips, drew her in, and kissed her. She moaned into his mouth and melted against him.

"Oh God," she said, against his mouth...

SEVEN

Vance Restin looked up when his houseman brought another man into his office.

"Mr. Peterson, sir," the houseman said.

"Thank you, Everett. You can go."

Everett, tall, grey-haired, remarkably fit for a man in his 60's, backed out of the room and left.

"Sit down, Peterson," Restin said.

Peterson sat. He wasn't Restin's foreman, but he was in charge of gunmen he hired.

"Did the message get delivered?"

"It did," Peterson said, "right to the clerk at Adams' hotel. Do you really think he'll come?"

"He stuck his nose where it didn't belong today," Restin said. "His curiosity will bring him here."

"And then?"

"You and your men will be ready."

"We're gonna kill him here?"

"That's not the plan," Restin said, "but I want you to be ready."

Before he could go any further someone else entered the room.

"Daddy!" Terry Restin said, peevishly. "How dare you—"

"Terry!" he roared. "How many times have I told you not to come bursting into my office?"

The pretty blonde put her hands on her hips and glared at her father.

"You can't scare me by yelling, Daddy. I don't work for you, you know."

Restin sighed, looked at Peterson, and said, "You can go. I'll talk to you and your men tomorrow morning."

"Yes, sir."

Peterson stood up and left.

"Close the door," Restin told his daughter.

"There's nobody else in the house!" she said.

"Everett is here."

"And you think you have secrets from him?" she asked, but she closed the door.

"Just sit down," Restin said. "Tell me what's on your mind...this time?"

"You know what's on my mind," she said. "I'm not going to Sacramento."

"Yes, you are," he said. "That's where you'll get the best education."

"I'm twenty years old, Daddy," she said. "I should be getting married, not going to college."

"After you've graduated you can marry anybody you want," he said. "Until then, any man who goes near you will have to deal with me."

She folded her arms and said, "I'm not going. You can't make me."

"I not only can make you," Restin said, "I'm going to have somebody take you."

"Who?"

"You'll see."

"One of your hired guns?"

"I said you'll see. Now why don't you go and do something with your hair or your nails? I have work to do."

26

"Daddy," she said, standing up, "you might send me there, or have somebody try to take me there, but I won't stay there."

"You'll stay," Restin said, "or you'll find your pockets empty, little girl."

"I'm not a little girl!"

"You're my little girl," he said, "until you graduate from college. Now go!"

She glared at him for a moment, then opened the door and stormed out, slamming it behind her.

*****

When Dave Peterson entered the bunkhouse his three partners looked up from their card game at one end of the room. At the other end the ranch hands ignored—or tried to ignore—Peterson and his gunnies. They did not approve of having to share their bunkhouse with the gun hands.

"Wanna sit in?" Hank Spenser asked him.

"Naw," Peterson said, but he did sit down with them. "Just talked to the boss."

"And?" Ted Banks said.

"He says Adams should be here tomorrow."

"We don't wanna kill Adams here," Stan Rhodes said. "Nobody'd see it. We wanna kill him in town." The other men nodded their agreement.

"We do what we get paid to do," Peterson reminded them.

"So we gotta kill him here?" Rhodes asked.

"We'll find out tomorrow," Peterson said. "Don't worry about it."

"You sure you don't wanna sit in here?" Spenser asked.

Peterson looked at the table, saw that most of the pennies were in front of Spenser.

"Yeah," he said, "okay." He stuck his hand in his pocket and came out with a handful of change. "Deal me in."

EIGHT

Beth sat on the edge of the bed with her hands in her lap.

"I want to watch you," she said.

"Watch me what?"

"Undress," she said. "I haven't watched a man undress in a long time."

"Well," he said, "who am I to deprive you?"

He unbuttoned his shirt, removed it, then undid his belt and trousers, let his pants drop to the floor, bunching around his ankles. He stepped out of them and kicked them away. Last, he slid his underwear down to his ankles and stepped out of them.

"Oh, my," she said, when he stood up. He didn't have to look down to know that he was fully erect. The sight and smell of her had done that to him, and kissing her had inflamed him even more.

"Come here," she said.

He stepped to her and stood in front of her. She ran her hands along the outside of his thighs, then the inside, and finally took his hard cock between her palms.

"It's so...pretty," she said. "My husband's is...well, ugly." She took it in her fist, moved her hand up and down. "It's so smooth. Ben's is...veiny. And it's...hot."

She leaned forward, pressed her cheek to his hot column of flesh.

"Oh yes," she said, rubbing him against her cheek. "I want to feel you."

"You are," he said, enjoying the sensation.

"No," she said, "in my mouth."

Before he could say anything she parted her lips and engulfed him. She slid him in and out of her mouth, enjoying the way his smooth, hot skin felt. As she continued he grew wetter and wetter, and started to move his hips in unison with the suction of her mouth.

"Mmmm," she moaned, sucking him more and more avidly. He reached down to take her breasts in his hands. Not only were they almost the size of ripe peaches, but they were as firm. His thumbs found the nipples hard, and flicked them, causing her to moan again.

"All right," he said, reaching down to grasp her beneath her arms, "up we go."

"Mmmmm, no," she said, as his penis slid from her mouth.

"Up on the bed," Clint said. "How much time do we have?"

She slid back on the bed and said, "A couple of hours."

"Where does your family think you are?"

"Working on a dress in the back of the general store," she said. "I often do that."

"All right then," he said, "there's no real hurry, is there?"

"I'm just...anxious."

He slid his hand over the flesh of her belly, felt it tremble.

"I can tell," he said.

She caught her breath as he moved his hand down lower, between her legs. He stroked her inner thighs, then moved his hand directly to her crotch. Her pubic hair was also honey-colored, but darkened because it was moist from her wet vagina. He touched her with his middle finger, causing her to gasp, and then slid his finger into her hot steaminess.

"Oh God," she said, arching her back.

He smiled at her, leaned down to kiss her breasts and nibble at her hard nipples while he moved his finger in and out of her.

He kissed her neck and shoulders, and then became impatient himself. Sliding down he positioned himself between her legs, removing his finger and replacing it with his tongue. As soon as the tip of his tongue touched her she gasped and arched her back again.

"Oh God," she said, as he continued to lick her, "yes, oh yes..."

He slid his hands beneath her to cup her buttocks and lifted her to his mouth. She had a taste all her own that he had never encountered with another woman, much like her smell. And, if anything, she grew even wetter, soaking his face and the sheet beneath them.

Finally, he withdrew and slid up over her, pressed the tip of his penis to her wetness. He had intended to enter her gently, but his own ardor caught up with him and he rammed his penis into her.

Her eyes went wide and she cried out, almost as if in pain.

"Are you all right?" he asked.

"Oh God," she said, wrapping her arms and legs around him, "I'm just fine!"

*****

Later they were lying in each other's arms when Clint said, "You have to leave soon."

"I know. But I don't want to."

"Your family is waiting."

She slid her hand down between his legs to grasp him. Immediately, he started to respond.

"I see you're not ready for me to go, either."

"Beth," he said, reaching down and grasping her hand, "this wasn't right to begin with. Let's not make it worse by having your husband come looking for you."

She brought her hand up from beneath the sheet with his and kissed the back of his.

"All right," she said, swinging her legs out of bed, "but we're going to do this again."

He watched as she got dressed, and she knew he was watching so she went slowly. By the time she was done he was fully hard again and ready to take her back into bed. He reached for her, but she skirted away.

"Oh, no," she said, "you're the one who made me get up. It's too late now."

She went to the door, then turned back to him.

"I'd kiss you goodbye, but I'm afraid you'd pull me back into bed."

"You're right."

"Get a good night's sleep," she said. "What are you doing tomorrow?"

He didn't want to tell her about the note from Restin, so he said, "I'm not sure."

"Then maybe I'll see you."

"Maybe."

She started to open the door, then asked, "You won't leave town without seeing me, will you?"

"I promise," he said, "I won't leave town without saying goodbye."

"That wasn't exactly what I had in mind," she said and slipped out of the room.

NINE

Clint woke in the morning, still unsure about whether or not to ride out to see Restin. He was, after all, a day or two away from leaving town for good. Why get involved in whatever Restin had in mind, because there was no way the man had asked him to come out to his ranch just to apologize. He had something on his mind.

After breakfast his curiosity got the better of him. He decided to saddle Eclipse and take a ride out to Restin's spread. If nothing else was accomplished, the Darley Arabian would get some exercise.

*****

He saddled Eclipse at the livery and asked the hostler for directions to the Restin spread.

"You better be careful out there," the old man told him.

"Why's that?"

"He not only has ranch hands, he's also got gun hands working for him." The man looked Clint up and down. "You ain't lookin' fer a job, are ya?"

"No, I'm not."

"Well, just watch your back out there, is all I'm sayin'," the man said. "Vance Restin is a hard man."

"Thanks for the advice."

He mounted up and rode out.

*****

The Restin spread was called the Bar-VR, which Clint thought didn't take a lot of imagination. Apparently, just two miles outside of town he crossed onto Restin land, but the house was still three miles beyond that.

He rode up to a two-story house—first story built of logs, and then the second floor added in rough-sawn lumber. There were some hands in the corral, working a good looking stallion, and nobody paid any attention to him from that direction.

However, there were two men on the porch that he recognized as two of the four gunmen from the day before. They were leaning and sitting, and as he rode up they straightened, their hands hanging down by their guns.

"You boys should relax," Clint said. "I'm here as an invited guest."

"That so?" one asked.

"Yeah, it is," Clint said. "Just ask him."

"Don't bother climbing down from that horse," the other man said.

Clint wondered if this was a trap, but he didn't sense that anyone was behind him, and he didn't think these two would face him alone.

"Why don't one of you run along inside and ask him," Clint suggested.

"I'll do that," the first man said. "Just stay there."

He went inside, leaving his partner to face Clint alone.

"Where are your other two friends?" Clint asked.

"They're around."

34

They had attracted some attention from the hands in the corral, but Clint still wasn't sensing any danger to him from behind.

The other man came out of the house and said, "The boss said to let him go inside."

Clint immediately dismounted.

"Don't think we're gonna take care of your horse," the first man said.

"He'll take care of himself," Clint said. He went up the steps until he was on equal ground with the two men, then stopped and looked at them. "He just better still be there when I come out."

He didn't wait for a response and entered the house.

Just inside the door he found the other two gunmen.

"Adams," one of them said, "I'm Peterson. Mr. Restin is this way."

Clint pointed at the other man.

"You're the one who recognized me," he said. "Who are you?"

"My name's Stan Rhodes."

"I don't know you."

"We've never met," Rhodes said, "but I saw you once, a while back."

"You wanna come this way?" Peterson asked. "The boss is waitin'."

"Peterson," Clint said. "And what's your first name?"

"Dave," Peterson said. "Don't worry, we don't know each other, and you never heard of me, either. You comin'?"

"Yeah," Clint said, "I'm coming. Lead the way."

Peterson took the lead and Rhodes followed behind, but Clint still didn't feel he was in danger. His instincts on that were usually good.

He followed Peterson to an impressive office, a large

room lined with books. Restin was seated behind a huge desk.

"Ah, Adams," the rancher said, "I'm glad you decided to stop by. You don't mind if Mr. Peterson and Mr. Rhodes stay with us, do you?"

"Not at all," Clint said, then added, "if you feel you need them."

"I'm sure a man like you understands about...precautions?" Restin asked. "Please, have a seat."

TEN

"Can I get you a drink? Or some coffee?"

"Nothing, thanks," Clint said. "I'm here to find out what's on your mind, Mr. Restin."

"Right to the point," Restin said. "Good. What's on my mind, Mr. Adams, is a job."

"A job?"

"A well paying job."

"Well," Clint said, "I'm not a ranch hand, and..." he looked around. "...I'm not a gun for hire."

"No, no," Restin said, "nothing like that, at all."

"Then what?"

"My daughter, Terry, is supposed to go to Sacramento to attend college," Restin said. "She doesn't want to go."

"How old is she?"

"Twenty."

"That seems old enough to make her own decisions."

"No!" Restin said. "She's my daughter, and I'll make the decisions for her. She's going to college to get a good education. After that she can do what she likes."

"What does this all have to do with me?"

"Ah," Restin said, with a smile, "you're the man who's going to see that she gets to Sacramento."

"And how do I do that?"

"Easy," Restin said, "you're going to take her there."

Clint was slightly stunned for a moment, then said

simply, "No."

"No?"

"Sorry," Clint said. "I'm not a babysitter."

"I didn't think you were," Restin assured him. "I was thinking of you as more of an...escort."

"That's not something I do either, Mr. Restin."

"I'll pay you a thousand dollars."

"No."

"Five thousand."

"Sorry."

Restin stood up angrily.

"I'm not used to being turned down, Adams."

Clint stood.

"Then you better get used to it."

Clint turned and headed for the door.

"Ten thousand!" Restin snapped.

Clint turned and said, "No."

"You're crazy."

"I don't work for men like you, Restin," Clint said, "at any price."

"Men like me?" Restin asked. "You mean rich and successful?"

"No," Clint said, "I mean arrogant."

Clint left the room and walked toward the front door.

"Boss?" Peterson said.

"Let him go," Restin said. "I'll just have to go to plan B."

"Plan B?" Rhodes asked. "Why not just pay us to do it?"

"As if I'd trust my daughter to you animals," Restin said. "No, I have something else in mind."

"So whataya want us to do?" Peterson asked.

"For the time being," Restin said, "nothing."

"So just let him go?"

Restin nodded. "That's right," he said. "Just let him go. Oh, and have my horse saddled."

"Where are we goin'?" Peterson asked.

"We're not going anywhere," Restin said, "but I'm going into town."

"You can't go alone."

"Nonsense," Restin said. "You just go out front and make sure those other two idiots don't do anything stupid."

*****

Clint went out the front door, ignored the two gunmen, and walked down the steps to Eclipse, who hadn't moved. He mounted up, turned the Darley Arabian, and rode away from the house.

The two gunmen exchanged an anxious glance, and then the door opened and Peterson came out. Stan Rhodes followed him out.

"We just gonna let 'im go?" Hank Spenser asked.

"That's exactly what we're gonna do."

"But...why?" Ted Banks demanded.

"Because that's what the boss wants us to do," Peterson said, "and he's payin' the bills."

Banks looked at Spenser, who shrugged and said, "What the hell? When we do get a chance at him maybe it'll be in town, where everybody can see."

Banks thought about that and then said, "Yeah, okay, I guess so."

"What'd the boss want with him?" Spenser asked.

"He offered him a job."

"One of our jobs?" Banks asked.

"No," Rhodes said, "somethin' else."

"And?" Spenser asked.

"Adams turned him down flat," Peterson said, "three different times."

"Ouch," Spenser said, "I'll bet Restin didn't like that."

"He kept offerin' him more money," Rhodes said, "got up to ten thousand."

"What?" Banks said. "That's more than we're gettin'! What the hell—"

"Never mind," Peterson said.

"Yeah," Spenser said, "what's the difference, if he turned it down. Maybe he'll pay us the ten thousand."

"I don't know," Peterson said. "He says he's got another plan."

"Like what?" Banks asked.

"That he didn't say," Rhodes said. "He's goin' into town. I gotta go and saddle his horse."

"We goin' with him?" Banks asked.

"No," Rhodes said, on his way down the steps, "he's goin' alone!"

"Alone?" Banks asked, looking at Peterson.

"He just thinks he's goin' alone," Peterson said. "After he mounts up and rides out you two go and saddle our horses—hurry!"

"We gonna follow him?" Banks asked.

"We're gonna follow him," Peterson said, nodding. "I'm not havin' our meal ticket gettin' shot."

ELEVEN

When Clint got back to Festus he put Eclipse back in the livery, in the capable hands of the old hostler.

"That didn't take long," the old man said.

"How long does it take to say no?"

"You said no to Vance Restin?"

"I did."

The old man cackled and shook his head. "He ain't gonna take kindly to that."

"What can he do about it?"

The old man shrugged. "He can put pressure on you in a lot of ways."

"How?" Clint said. "I don't have any family or friends in this town. There's just me."

"Well," the man said, "he'll figure somethin' out. Just wait and see."

"I won't hold my breath, old man," Clint said. "See to my horse."

"I'll take good care of 'im."

Clint left the livery and went to the saloon.

*****

Moments behind Clint, Vance Restin rode into town on a majestic Palomino. He reined in the horse in front of the sheriff's office and went inside.

41

"Moreland!" he snapped. "We need to talk."

The sheriff had been talking with his young deputy. When he saw Vance Restin in his office he said, "Go do your rounds, Billy."

"Yes, sir."

As Billy headed for the door he said, "Hello, Mr. Restin," but the rancher ignored him.

"What's on your mind, Mr. Restin?" Moreland asked, seating himself behind his desk.

"Clint Adams."

"What about him?" the sheriff asked. "I understand he's gonna leave town soon, so you won't have any problems with him anymore. I hope you're not plannin' on sending your gunnies after him. You just might end up having to hire more."

"No, no," Restin said, waving the sheriff's words away. "I don't want Adams dead. I want him working for me."

"Did you make him an offer?"

"I did."

"And?"

"He turned me down flat."

"Ooh," Moreland said, "that must've made you mad."

"You have no idea."

"And you don't want to kill him?"

"No."

"Then what do you want?"

Restin looked around, his eyes stopping at the coffee pot on the pot-bellied stove.

"Give me a cup of coffee and I'll tell you."

*****

Just minutes behind Vance Restin, Peterson and his three gunnies rode into town.

"There's his Palomino," he said. "In front of the Sheriff's office."

"What the hell," Rhodes said. "What's he doin' talkin' to the law?"

"That's his business," Peterson said. "I just want to keep him alive so he can keep payin' us."

"So whatta we do?" Banks asked.

"Hide the horses," Peterson said. "We don't want him to know we're here. Then we'll all find a place to hide ourselves and watch his back."

They all dismounted and gave Banks their reins.

"Hide 'em where?" Banks asked.

"Use your imagination," Peterson said.

TWELVE

Clint was leaning over a beer in the half empty saloon when the Sheriff walked in with his deputy.

"Sheriff," he said. "Join me?"

"No, Mr. Adams," Moreland said, "I need you to join me."

"Where?"

Both star packers drew their guns, Billy doing so very nervously. Clint let them, because he instinctively knew they weren't about to shoot him.

"What's going on, Sheriff?"

"Just stand still," Moreland said. He looked at the bartender. "Louie, get his gun."

"What the—" the bartender started.

"Just do it!"

The barman reached over the bar and plucked Clint's gun from his holster, saying, "Sorry, Mr. Adams."

"Don't worry about it, Louie."

"Now let's take a walk to the jail," Moreland said.

"No explanation?" Clint asked.

"You'll get your explanation once we get there." He waggled his gun barrel. "Move!"

*****

When they got to the jail, Clint was surprised to be

put right into a cell.

"What's going on, Sheriff?" he demanded.

"Well, right now you're in a cell," Moreland said. "That means I gotta feed ya."

"Don't worry about that," Clint said, "just tell me—" but the sheriff was gone, closing the door of the cellblock behind him. Clint was alone to ponder the three walls and bars of his cell.

*****

Sheriff Moreland went over to the Drinkwater Saloon, which was where Vance Restin did his drinking when he was in town—mostly because he owned the place. It was small, expensively put together, and most of the townspeople didn't like it much, so they didn't patronize it. That suited Restin just fine. He didn't even let his own men go into the Drinkwater.

Moreland found him sitting at his usual table near the front window. The bartender, a tall, dour looking man in his forties named Buck, was wiping down the bar with a dry rag—dry because the bar never got wet, because nobody ever went inside.

"Buck," Restin said, "bring the sheriff a beer."

"Yes, sir."

"Sit down, Moreland."

The Sheriff sat and Buck set a beer in front of him. Restin had a bottle of whiskey and a glass, poured himself a shot.

"You get him?"

"I did."

"Any problem?"

"No," Moreland said, "he came peaceful."

"So he's in a cell?"

46

"Yep."

"Well, let him stew for a while," Restin said, "and then tell him what he's being charged with."

"Can I feed him?"

"Sure."

"And after I charge him?"

"Tell me how he reacts."

"And then what?"

Restin drank his drink and poured himself another glass. The sheriff took the opportunity to drink some beer.

"And then we'll move onto the next step."

"And after that?"

"I'll offer him a job again," Restin said. "I think he'll take it, then, don't you?"

THIRTEEN

When the cellblock door opened, the Sheriff appeared carrying a tray covered by a cloth napkin.

"Got your lunch," he said to Clint.

"I'd rather have some answers."

"I got those, too," the Sheriff said, "but you better eat first."

There was a cut-out in the cell bars where the tray could be pushed through. Clint accepted it, mainly because he was hungry.

"Something to drink?"

"I'll get you some water."

"I'd rather have coffee."

"Okay."

While the Sheriff went for the coffee, Clint uncovered the tray, found a plate with fried chicken and potatoes. He had a fork, but no knife. That was okay. He picked up the chicken with his hands and speared the potatoes with the fork.

The Sheriff came in, handed him a tin cup of coffee through the bars.

"Thanks. This is pretty good."

"Yeah, comes from a good café down the street." He turned to leave.

"Why not stay?" Clint asked. "We can talk while I eat."

"Naw," Moreland said. "A man should be left alone to eat in peace."

He turned to leave, and Clint let him go without objection this time. The sheriff would tell him what this was all about soon enough.

He decided to relax and enjoy his free lunch.

*****

A couple of hours later, Clint was lying on his back on his cot when the cellblock door slammed open and Moreland came walking in.

"Okay, Adams, stand up," he said.

Clint sat up. "What now?"

"Just stand up."

Clint stood.

"Mrs. Nolan?" Moreland said, looking at someone outside the cellblock.

A middle-aged woman came walking into the cell-block timidly, flinching as if she was waiting to be hit.

"Now take your time, Meg," Moreland said. "Take a good long look."

The woman raised her eyes to look at Clint, then quickly looked away. Clint had a sudden inkling as to what was going on, and he felt that this woman was not here of her own free will.

"Is this him?" Moreland asked. "Is this the man you saw shoot your husband?"

Meg Nolan reluctantly lifted her eyes and looked at Clint again. He thought he saw apology in her eyes.

"Y-yes," she said, "that's him."

"You have to say it, Meg," the sheriff told her.

"T-that's the man who shot my husband."

"All right, then," Moreland said. He put his arms

around the woman and turned her. "That's all, Meg."

She walked out.

Moreland turned to face Clint.

"I get it now," Clint said.

"Get what?"

"This is a frame," he said. "A put-up job. You put her up to identifying me as the man who shot her husband. If he was even really shot. Is he dead? Or just wounded? Did you actually have someone shot in order to make it stick?"

"I don't know what you're talkin' about, Adams," Moreland said. "It's not unusual for you to shoot a man, is it?"

"I don't know what the game is, Sheriff," Clint said, "but I'm thinking you'll let me know, sooner or later." He sat down on his cot. "All I have to do is be patient and wait."

Moreland stared at Clint for a moment, then turned and walked out, closing the cellblock door behind him.

*****

Moments later he was back in the Drinkwater Saloon, sitting across from Restin again.

"Well?"

"She identified him."

"And?"

"He knows something's up," Moreland said. "That it's a put-up job."

"He thinks it is," Restin corrected him.

"Yes."

"What did he say?"

"He's gonna be patient," the lawman said, "and wait until I tell him what's goin' on."

"He's good," Restin said. "I'm impressed. But he'll have to go along. He won't have a choice, will he?"

"What if he wants to see a body?" Moreland asked. "What if he wants to see the man he's supposed to have shot?"

Vance Restin poured himself another drink—same bottle as before—and said, "Then we'll give him one."

FOURTEEN

oreland came in that evening with another tray.

"Supper," he said.

"From the same place?"

"Yes."

"Good," Clint said. He accepted the tray. "Some more coffee?"

"I'll bring it."

Clint sat down, took the napkin off the tray. Steak this time. He was glad. At least he was eating well.

Moreland came in with the coffee and handed it to him.

"Thanks." He walked to his cot, sat down, set the coffee cup down, and picked up the tray. This time he had a knife and fork.

"Can you tell me how long this will take?" Clint asked.

"We have to wait for the circuit judge."

"A town this size has no judge?"

"He died. We haven't been able to replace him yet."

"Very convenient."

Moreland didn't comment.

"Can you stay while I eat and talk?" Clint asked.

"Naw," Moreland said, "a man—"

"Yeah, I know," Clint said, "should be left alone to eat in peace."

"Just let me know when you're done," Moreland said, and left.

*****

Harry Ballard ran into the house and said, "Clint's been arrested."

"What?" Beth said.

"What do you mean arrested?" Ben asked. "For what?"

"I dunno," the boy said. "All I know is, he's in the jail."

"How do you know?" Ben asked.

"I was in the café when the sheriff came in to buy a steak dinner for his prisoner," Harry said. "He told the lady the prisoner was the Gunsmith. That's what they call Clint, ain't it? The Gunsmith?"

"Yes, that's what they call him," Ben said.

"We have to do something," Beth said to her husband.

"What can we do?" he asked.

"I don't know," she said, "but he has no friends in town."

"How do you know that?"

"Never mind that, Ben," she said. "Do something."

"There's nothing I can do—"

"Oh God," she said, grabbing her shawl from a hook on the wall, "you're hopeless. Stay with Harry!"

She stormed out the door.

*****

Moments later Beth stormed into the sheriff's office.

"Sheriff, do you have Clint Adams in a cell?"

"Mrs. Ballard," Moreland said, "that's no concern of you—"

"I assume that means yes," she said. "What have you arrested him for?"

"That's none of your business."

"Well...let him out," she said. "I'll pay his bail."

"No bail yet, Ma'am," Moreland said. "We're waitin' on the circuit judge."

"How long will that take?"

Moreland shrugged.

"Who knows?"

"Then let me talk to him."

"Why?"

"Why not?" she asked. "Are you afraid I'll break him out of your jail?"

"Of course not."

"Then where's the harm in letting me talk to him?" she asked.

He stared at her for a few moments, then shrugged and said, "Well, what the hell? Okay. Come on."

He walked her to the door of the cellblock, unlocked it and said, "Five minutes."

"Fine."

She went in.

*****

Clint was lying on his back on the cot, his left arm across his forehead, when she said, "Clint?"

He jerked up and looked at her.

"Beth?" He sat up. "What are you doing here?"

She came close to the bars. "I heard you were arrested."

"How?"

"Harry was at the café when the sheriff picked up your supper."

He approached the bars and she took his hand.

"What did he arrest you for?"

"I don't know," Clint said. "He hasn't really told me yet but...do you know a woman named Meg Nolan?"

"Of course I know Meg," she said. "I make dresses for her."

"Well, he dragged her in here and had her identify me as the man who shot her husband."

"Ed was shot?"

"Who is Ed Nolan?"

"Just a merchant here in town," she said. "Runs the hardware store. Why would anybody shoot him? Why would you shoot him?"

"I didn't," Clint said. "In fact, I don't even know if he was really shot. Hey, maybe you could find out for me."

"Well," she said, "I tried to bail you out and couldn't. I'd like to help you, somehow."

"Great. See if you can find out if good ol' Ed has even been shot."

"Why would they arrest you for shootin' him if he wasn't shot?"

"And why would she identify me if he wasn't shot?" Clint asked. "Those are good questions."

"Are they...framin' you?"

"It sure sounds like it," Clint said, "but maybe there's really no crime to frame me for. That's the first thing I'd like to know."

"I'll try and find out."

"But don't try to come back here tonight," he said. "I don't want you to get into trouble. Come back in the morning."

"I'll arrange with the sheriff for me to bring you breakfast," she suggested.

"That's a great idea,' Clint said, "but tell him you'll bring him some, too."

"Why should I feed him?"

"Because then he'll let you in."

"Ah, I see," she said. "Okay. I'll do it."

He squeezed her hand and said, "Thanks, Beth."

She squeezed back and said, "I'll see you in the morning."

As she left, Clint realized how good it felt to actually have somebody on his side.

FIFTEEN

He woke early with the sun streaming through the barred window. At least there was no hammering. Nobody was building a gallows outside his cell.

Not yet, anyway.

He heard something outside the cellblock, and then the key in the lock. When the door opened Beth came walking in with a tray.

"The sheriff says I have to slide it through here to you," she said, putting it through the slot.

"That's fine."

"It's ham and eggs, he wouldn't let me include a knife," she went on.

"Also okay."

"He has coffee outside. I'll get it for you."

"Thanks."

He started eating and she brought in the coffee and handed it to him.

"Did you give the sheriff his breakfast?"

"I did."

"Can you stay?"

"He said I can."

"All right, then." He lowered his voice. "Did you talk to Mrs. Nolan? Was her husband shot?"

"She says he was," Beth said, "but..."

"But what?"

59

"I don't believe she's tellin' the truth," Beth said. "I think she's lyin'."

"Did you see him?"

"No," Beth said, "she wouldn't let me."

"Then she probably is lying," Clint said. "That's good."

"It is?"

"Yes," he said. "It means nobody has really been shot. I think I've got this figured out."

"What do you think is happenin'?"

"I'll tell you later," he said. "If I'm right, this will probably all be resolved sometime today."

"So you're satisfied to sit here and wait?"

"Yes."

She took a deep breath.

"Well, all right," she said, "if you say so."

"You should just go and be with your family, Beth," Clint said. "Tell Harry I said hi, and that everything will be just fine."

"All right," she said.

He finished eating and passed the tray back to her.

"Can you get me some more coffee before you go?"

"Of course."

Beth went out and came back with another cup of coffee.

"Thanks. Now go back to your family and relax. I'll be seeing you soon."

"Are you sure?"

"Fairly sure."

"All right, then." Still unconvinced, she left.

Clint drank his coffee and went over the matter again in his mind. There was only one reason he could think this was happening, and that was because he turned down a job from Vance Restin. If he was right, he'd be seeing Restin very soon.

*****

Vance Restin entered the Sheriff's office later that afternoon.

"Moreland," he said, "how's our guest doing?"

"He's remarkably calm," the lawman said. "Not complaining at all, not asking any questions."

"Is that right?" Restin didn't like that. "What do you think is going on?"

"He's a smart man," Moreland said. "He might have figured this out."

"That doesn't matter," Restin said. "Whether he figured it out or not, he's in jail until I say so."

"Maybe he should know that," Moreland said.

"I'm about to go in and tell him," the rancher said.

SIXTEEN

When Vance Restin entered the cellblock Clint knew he'd figured it correctly. Now he had to play it right.

"Mr. Adams," Restin said. "I hope the sheriff is making you comfortable in here?"

"Very," Clint said. "I'm being fed very well."

"That's good," Restin said. "I suppose you'd like to know what you're being charged with."

"I was assuming the sheriff would let me know," Clint replied. "I didn't expect to hear it from you."

"Well," Restin said, "the situation is sort of...unique."

"In what way?"

"In the way that I could make it go away, if I wanted to," the man said.

"Wait," Clint said, "I assume I'm being charged with...what? Shooting someone?"

"Assault," Restin said, "and attempted murder."

"Of a man I don't even know."

"I'm sure a man like you is used to shooting men you don't know," Restin said.

"That's not strictly true," Clint said. "I try not to shoot anyone unless I'm forced into it."

"As I understand it," Restin said, "Ed Nolan had no chance against you. There's such a thing as a man being totally overmatched."

"Well, I can't comment on that since I've never even

63

seen the man I'm supposed to have shot."

"Well, there's a witness—"

"His wife," Clint said, cutting him off, "who I'm sure has been forced to say what you want her to say."

"That's entirely possible," Restin said.

Clint was surprised that the rancher admitted it.

"And she can be convinced to unsay it."

"So you're saying that you can arrange for me to walk out of here free and clear?"

"Exactly."

"And all I have to do is...what? Take your daughter to Sacramento?"

Restin smiled.

"I knew you were a smart man," he said. "Yes, all you have to do is accept the job I offered you."

"At the same pay rate? Ten thousand?"

"Five."

"I thought the last offer was ten."

"It was," Restin said, "but now the offer is five— payable at the other end when you deliver her to the University."

This was exactly what Clint had been expecting. The only thing was, he hadn't figured a way out of it.

"And if you go part way and decide to run off," Restin went on, "the charges will be refiled and a wanted poster will be issued for you. You'll be a man on the run."

"You're a sonofabitch, you know that?"

"Of course I know it," Restin said. "So what's your answer?"

"I have to think about it."

"Still thinking you can come up with a way out?" Restin asked, and then didn't give Clint a chance to reply. "Sure, go ahead and think about it. You have until tomorrow morning, and then the charges stick. You'll be sitting in here until the circuit judge comes to town."

"I'll let you know tomorrow," Clint said.

"Think long and hard, my friend," Restin said. "I'm not a man you want to cross."

With that Restin turned and walked out.

*****

"What happened?" Sheriff Moreland asked the rancher as he came out of the cellblock.

"He wants to think about it."

"He's in a cell, charged with murder, and he wants to think about it?"

"I gave him until morning and then I told him the charges stick."

"How do you intend to make these charges stick when nobody's really been shot?" Moreland asked.

"Don't worry about it, Sheriff," the rancher said. "That'll be my problem. I'll see you tomorrow."

As Restin left, Moreland couldn't believe that the man would really have Ed Nolan shot in order to make these charges stick. If that was the case, would he be able to go along with it?

He poured two cups of coffee and carried them into the cellblock.

"Coffee?" he asked Clint.

"Thanks."

Moreland passed the cup through the bars.

"This guy is really serious, isn't he?" Clint asked Moreland.

"I'm afraid so."

"And you're going to go along with it?"

"I like my job."

"What if he decided to really shoot this Nolan fella

just so he can charge me with the crime?"

Moreland didn't answer.

"Ha!" Clint said. "You were just thinking the same thing, weren't you?"

"Maybe," Sheriff Moreland said, "you might want to talk to a lawyer."

SEVENTEEN

When the lawyer walked into the cellblock he did not fill Clint with a lot of confidence. For one thing, he was eating a sandwich and had crumbs down the front of his suit. And for another, the suit had seen better days.

Was the sheriff digging his grave deeper with this recommendation? Moreland did strike Clint as a man who loved his job, but hated his situation. He supposed he'd have to give this fellow a chance.

"Mr. Adams?" the man asked.

"That's right," Clint said. "And you're Eugene Barkley?"

"That's right."

"You're kind of...young."

"I'm very young," Barkley said, "and I'm broke. I need a case, and you need a lawyer." The young man shrugged. "It's a match made in heaven."

"Maybe..."

Barkley stood just outside the cell holding a leather briefcase, staring at Clint.

"Do I stay or do I go?"

"Stay," Clint said. "We'll talk."

*****

After fifteen minutes Eugene Barkley looked at Clint and said, "You need help."

"That's why you're here."

"No," the lawyer said, "you need a lot of help."

"Are you telling me you're not the one to give me that help?" Clint asked.

"Well, now, that depends."

"On what?"

"Can you pay me?"

"Of course I can pay you."

"Then like you said, "Barkley said, "let's talk..."

Clint explained his predicament to Barkley, who listened intently without interrupting.

"I don't get it," he said, when Clint was done.

"What don't you get?"

"Why don't you take the job, deliver the girl, and accept the five thousand dollars?"

"I don't want to work for Vance Restin," Clint said.

"Maybe he'd let me deliver her, then."

"Why don't you ask him?" Clint suggested. "Maybe that would get me out of here."

"Maybe," Barkley said, "we should look into some legal way of getting you out of here."

"So you'll take my case?"

"I will," Barkley said. "But you should probably take my advice."

"Which is?"

"Do the job," Barkley said, "and while you're doing it, I'll be here working on our defense."

"If I do the job," Clint said, "I won't need you to work on my defense."

"Do you really think Vance Restin will drop the charges even if you do the job?" Barkley asked. "If you do you're more naïve than I would've thought a man of your caliber would be."

"If I don't come back here after I deliver the girl," Clint said, "--and that's if I do the job—if I don't come back here, what could he do?"

"I'm sure you'd have some wanted posters out on you in no time," Barkley said. "I think this battle has to be fought on two fronts, Mr. Adams."

Clint was starting to think that Eugene Barkley might be right. Vance Restin was not a man who could be trusted.

"Okay, then," he said, "let's talk about that."

*****

After the young lawyer left, Sheriff Moreland came into the cellblock.

"The kid said you wanted to see me."

"Yes," Clint said. "First, I wanted to thank you for recommending him to me."

"Me?" Moreland said. "Did I do that? I don't remember."

"Yeah, well, that's fine," Clint said. "Anyway, take a message to your boss."

"My boss is the mayor of the town."

"Then take a message to your town's number one citizen," Clint said.

"And what would that message be?"

"Tell him...I'll take the job," Clint said. "Five thousand dollars to deliver his daughter to a university in Sacramento."

"Five thousand, huh?" He didn't move.

"Are you looking for a cut?" Clint asked.

"Naw," Moreland said, "just wonderin' what my price would be to give up my job."

"Five thousand dollars for a hunk of time," Clint said. "What do you think?"

Moreland touched his badge, thought a moment, then said, "I'll deliver your message."

EIGHTEEN

"**Y**ou're out of here!"

Sheriff Moreland came walking into the cell-block, keys jangling. He inserted the key into the lock of Clint's cell and swung the door open.

"Just like that?"

"Come outside."

The Sheriff left the cellblock. Clint picked up his hat and followed. Moreland had put his gun belt on top of his desk.

"I gave Mr. Restin your message," he said. "He wants to see you."

"Out at his ranch?"

"No," Moreland said. "A saloon called the Drinkwater, here in town."

"When?"

"Today," the lawman said. "Right away, if you can."

"I can't," Clint said. "I need a hot bath and a shave, first."

"You're gonna keep him waitin'?"

"Sure," Clint said, strapping on his gun, "why not?"

*****

Clint went to his hotel, where he still had his room. He arranged with the clerk for a hot bath, then got some fresh clothes from his saddlebags.

After the bath he felt almost human again. Even one night behind bars was enough to make a man feel like an animal. He crossed the street to a barbershop and got himself a shave and a trim. When he stepped back out on the street, he felt like himself again.

He headed for the Drinkwater Saloon.

*****

Vance Restin sat opposite his man, Peterson.

"You think I didn't know you and your men followed me to town yesterday?"

"Just lookin' out for you, Boss."

"That's what I pay you for. That's why I brought you to town with me, today."

Stan Rhodes came running over from the batwing doors.

"He's comin' down the street!"

"All right," Restin told them, "get out. Go out the back way."

"But Boss—"

"Go!" Restin said. "He's not going to kill me."

Peterson stood and jerked his head at Rhodes to follow him. The other two gunnies were somewhere else, probably a whorehouse.

"Buck!"

"Yeah, Boss?"

"When Adams sits down bring him a beer."

"Sure, Boss."

"You still got that shotgun behind the bar?"

"Yep."

"Keep an eye on him," Restin said. "If I'm wrong and he kills me, you kill him."

"Sure, Boss."

Restin sat back and poured himself a drink from the bottle on the table. He picked it up and waited.

*****

Clint approached the little saloon, looked around. People were walking by, but nobody went in or came out of the saloon.

When he stepped inside he saw that the place was empty except for Restin and the bartender. He walked to Restin's table.

"Have a seat," the rancher said. "I'm sure you could use a beer."

Clint sat. The bartender came over with a cold mug of beer.

"You got a shotgun behind that bar?" he asked the man.

The barman looked at Restin.

"He does," Restin said.

"He won't need it."

Restin waved the man back to the bar. "That's good to hear," he said. "The Sheriff tells me you've decided to accept my offer."

"How could I refuse?"

"Exactly."

"What do we do first?"

"First, you have to meet my daughter."

"And how do we do that?"

"You'll come to my house for supper tonight," Restin said. "I'll introduce you."

"Why does she need to be taken to Sacramento?" Clint asked. "Isn't she old enough to go on her own?"

"She is," Restin said, "but she won't. She doesn't

want to go. You're going to have to make her."

"Great," Clint said. "Will she be kicking and screaming the whole way?"

"I guess that'll be up to you," Restin said. "I will say this. She's not an easy girl to handle."

Clint picked up his beer and drank down half of it morosely.

"Relax," Restin said. "Maybe she'll like you."

NINETEEN

After Clint agreed to ride out to Restin's ranch to meet his daughter and have supper, he walked to his young lawyer's office on one of the town's side streets.

"You're out," the young lawyer said happily as Clint entered his small, cramped office.

"I'm out," Clint said. He looked around for a place to sit.

Barkley got up from his desk to move some files from a chair so Clint could sit.

"I was under the impression you didn't have a lot of cases," he said, looking around at the clutter.

"Not like yours," Barkley said. "Most of this is just filing, lots of paperwork. Your case is different. Did you meet with Mr. Restin?"

"Yes," Clint said. "I accepted his job, for five thousand dollars."

"Delivering his daughter to the University in Sacramento?" Barkley asked.

"Yes."

"Good," the lawyer said. "When do you leave?"

"I don't know," Clint said. "I'm supposed to go out to his ranch tonight for supper and meet the girl."

"I understand she's...difficult."

"That's what he said. Have you met her?"

"I've seen her, but I haven't met her," Barkley said.

"She's a lovely girl."

"I've heard that, too. Do you know if she has a boy-friend in town?"

"Not that I've heard."

"Maybe one of her father's hands? Or gunnies?"

"Nope. Unless she's doing it on the sly."

Clint sat back in his chair.

"What's bothering you?"

"I just don't think I'm being told the whole truth," Clint said. "Why does this girl need to be escorted to Sacramento? Is somebody going to try to stop her?"

"Don't you think he'd tell you that?"

"I think he should tell me that," Clint answered, "but maybe he's not."

"Maybe you should take somebody with you," the lawyer said. "You know, somebody to watch your back."

"Are you volunteering?"

"Me?" The lawyer shook his head. "I can't shoot, and I'd never be able to stay in the saddle all the way to Sacramento."

"I don't know anybody else in town."

"You can't hire somebody for that job?"

"I can't have somebody watching my back if I don't know them."

"I guess I can see that."

"But I might be able to get somebody to meet me somewhere along the way. But I'll have to send some telegrams."

"Meanwhile," Eugene Barkley said, "I'll be working on your case, trying to make sure Restin can't go back on your deal."

"You'll need some money," Clint said.

"Yes, I will."

"I'll have to go to the bank first thing in the morning."

"You have money in the local bank?"

"I'll have to send it by wire," Clint said, "transferred into the bank in your name. Is that okay?"

"That's fine," Barkley said. "Money's money."

Clint stood up.

"I can send my telegrams now so it'll be done by morning," Clint said. "And maybe I can find myself some back-up."

"I hope so," Barkley said, standing. "Just come and see me in the morning and let me know what's going on. And what happens at the Restin ranch tonight."

"All right. Do you want to tell me where you live?"

"Right here, for now," Barkley said. "It's cheaper to live and work in the same place. For now."

*****

Clint went looking for the telegraph office, found it on the main street. He sent several telegrams, only one of which was to a bank.

He told the clerk what hotel he was at.

"I'll bring the replies over there, sir."

Clint handed him some extra money and said, "As they come in, all right? Don't wait for them all to come in so you can bring them at one time."

"Yessir," the clerk said, happily pocketing the extra money.

Clint left the telegraph office and went to the Drink-water Saloon. He peered inside over the batwing doors, saw that nobody was there but Buck, the bartender. He went in.

Buck looked up from the bar in surprise, as if shocked that anyone would walk in off the street.

"You don't do much business around here, do you?"

Clint asked.

The man shrugged.

"I get paid whether I pour drinks or not."

"Care to pour me one?"

"Sure."

"Beer."

Buck nodded, drew the beer, and set it down in front of Clint.

"No charge, according to the boss."

"The boss?"

"Mr. Restin owns this place."

That didn't surprise Clint. "Figures."

"Look, friend," Buck said, "Want my advice?"

"Sure," Clint said, "a bartender's advice is always welcome."

"Do the job, take the money, and don't come anywhere near here again."

"That does sound like good advice." Clint drank down the beer. "Does your boss keep his word?"

"If it means money to him."

"Otherwise?"

Buck shrugged.

"Thanks."

"Sure."

Clint left the saloon and went to the livery to saddle Eclipse.

He had a supper to attend.

TWENTY

"**A**re you ready?" Restin asked.

His daughter turned and looked at him.

"Can't I even have some privacy in my own room?"

"Our guest will be here soon."

"Then go on downstairs, Daddy," she said. "I'll be along in a minute."

"You look fine now."

"Daddy!"

He pointed his finger at her.

"Don't make me have to come up and get you," he said, "or send somebody."

"Like one of your gunmen?"

"Just come down," Restin said, "like a good girl."

She turned to face him, hands behind her back and said, "Yes, Daddy."

*****

This time when he rode up to the house there were no hands in the corral and no gunmen on the porch. But as he started up the steps the front door opened and a tall man stepped out.

"You must be Adams," he said.

"I must be."

"I'll have somebody see to your horse."

"I don't think he needs to be unsaddled."

"We'll just put him in the barn and feed him."

"Okay, thanks. You're not one of Restin's gunnies, are you?"

"I'm the foreman," the man said, "whatever that means anymore." He stuck his hand out. "Ray Owens."

"Clint Adams." Clint shook his hand.

"Actually, if you want my advice, you'll mount back up and ride out. Keep ridin'."

"That's good advice," Clint said, "if I didn't think the West would be wallpapered with wanted posters if I did that."

"Yeah, you're probably right. Go on in, then. They're waitin' for you. I'll see to your horse."

"You going to come in and eat?"

"They don't eat with the help," Owens said.

The man appeared to be in his thirties, looked as if he'd earned his way up to foreman.

"Why don't you take your own advice?" Clint asked. "I mean, if you feel the way you do."

"I doubt I could find a job that would pay me this good," Owens said. "I'll put up with a lot as long as I can." Owens waved. "Go."

Clint handed the man Eclipse's reins and went inside.

As he entered he saw a girl coming down a wide staircase, dark hair cascading down around her blue dress. She stopped short when she saw him.

"You must be him," she said.

"Who's that?"

She shrugged.

"I don't even know what to call you. My babysitter? My...deliverer?"

"How about for now," he said, "you just call me

Clint?"

"Well, Clint." She came down the steps the rest of the way and put out her hand. "I'm Terry."

He shook her hand, thinking this was not what he'd expected from all he had heard.

"Oh, I know what you're thinking," she said. "You were expecting some kind of hellcat."

"Well...yeah."

"Why don't we go in to supper and I'll show you what kind of a hellcat I can be?" She took his arm. "Daddy's waiting."

TWENTY-ONE

As they entered the dining room together Vance Restin stood up from his place at the head of the table.

"Look who I found, Daddy."

"Ah, there you are, Mr. Adams," he said, expansively. "And you've met my Terry."

"Yes, I have," Clint said. "She seems like a lovely young woman."

"She is, she is. Please, have a seat and we'll start the meal. Terry?"

"Daddy likes me to sit at his right," Terry said. "You should sit on his left."

She released Clint's arm and went to sit down. Her father held her chair for her, and then sat down himself. Clint walked around the table and sat on Restin's left.

A woman came out of the kitchen carrying trays of food and set them down on the table. Clint had been served like this before in other homes. But it had never made him this uncomfortable before.

"Go ahead, Mr. Adams," Restin said. "Help yourself."

"Yes, Mr. Adams," Terry said, politely, "please."

"Ladies first," Clint said.

"Oh," she said, "a gentleman." She looked at her father. "What a nice change."

Clint took a large chicken breast from the platter in

the center of the table, then vegetables from each of the others. The food was delicious.

"You have a good cook," he said.

"She's the best," Restin said, "and I pay her like the best."

"Daddy pays all his people like the best," Terry said. "Don't you, Daddy?"

"I pay everyone what they're worth," the rancher said, filling his own plate, "and I expect them to earn every penny."

"Like your foreman?" Clint asked.

"Ray? What do you know about him?"

"I met him out front."

"Ray's been with me a long time."

"Is he in charge of all the men?" Clint asked. "The hands, the gunnies? Or just the hands?"

"Ray handles the day-to-day business of the ranch," Restin said, "and that's all."

"Ray is Daddy's right hand when it comes to the ranch," Terry said. "For the other stuff he has Mr. Peterson."

"Yes," Clint said, "I've met Peterson, too. And his boys."

"Now they," Terry said, while chewing a small bite of chicken, "are not gentlemen."

"Honey," Restin said, "Mr. Adams—""Let's call him Clint, Daddy," Terry said. "Is that all right, Clint?"

"That's fine, Terry."

"All right, then," Restin said. "Terry, Clint is here so you and he can get acquainted. You'll be spending some time together between here and Sacramento. You should get to know each other."

"And that's what we're doing," she said, with a smile. "Getting to know each other. Aren't we, Clint?"

"That's exactly what we're doing."

"So tell me, Clint," she asked, "how did you get to be a legend?"

"You don't get to be a legend," Clint said. "People just start calling you one."

"And the name sticks?"

"I'm afraid so."

"And then...what?" she asked. "You have to start trying to live up to it?"

"That's the general idea."

"What a terrible place to live," she said. "Men must be coming after you all the time, to make a name for themselves."

"Men," he said, "boys..."

"And you killed them?"

"Some of them."

She looked at Restin.

"Daddy, do you think this is a good idea?"

"What's that, honey?"

"Well, for me to travel with the Gunsmith?" she asked. "What if somebody comes after him to challenge him and shoots me by mistake?"

"I trust Clint to take very good care of you, Terry," Restin said. "You're not getting out of going to college that easily."

"Ooooh!" she growled. She stood up and slammed her fist down on the tabletop, causing all the platters to jump and the gravy boat to spill. "I won't go! You can't make me..." she said, and then, pointing at Clint, "...and he can't make me go, either!"

She stormed out of the dining room.

"Jeanette!" he called.

The middle-aged cook came from the kitchen and asked, "Yes, sir?"

Restin pointed to the upended gravy boat and said, "We need more gravy."

TWENTY-TWO

Over coffee and pie Restin said, "I told you she wouldn't cooperate."

"Well, she had me fooled," Clint said. "From the moment I walked in she was nothing but sweet."

"Believe me, Terry is anything but sweet."

"Who does she take after?" Clint asked.

"Believe it or not, her mother."

"Is her mother alive?"

"No," Restin said, "she died a lot of years ago."

"And you never remarried?"

"No. It was difficult—with a daughter like Terry, women—it was hard. So I concentrated on building up my business."

"Seems like you did a hell of a job."

"I may not have been a perfect husband or father, Adams," Restin said, "but even if I say so myself, I'm a perfect money maker."

"Well," Clint said, "if you've got to be something..."

"Come on," Restin said, "it may be a cliché, but I like a cigar on the porch after supper."

They stood and Clint followed him out. Eclipse wasn't where he'd left him. He figured the big Darley Arabian was in the barn where Ray Owens said he'd take him.

The corral was still empty as Restin lit up a cigar and

offered one to Clint.

"That's a good cigar," Clint said. "Don't waste it on me."

Restin nodded, put the extra one back in his cigar holder, and lit one up. He did it lovingly, holding the flame to the tip and rotating the cigar until he had it going exactly the way he wanted.

"What's the game, Restin?" Clint asked.

"Huh?" Restin tore his attention away from the cigar. "What are you talking about? What game?"

"This can't just be about taking your daughter to college in Sacramento," Clint said. "As difficult as she might be."

"She's mighty difficult."

"Not five thousand dollars worth," I said. "Or ten. That was your last offer, wasn't it? Ten?"

"I would've gone to twenty," he said. "That's my daughter. I love her, Mr. Adams. I want her to have a good life, in spite of herself."

"Why is she so against it?"

"Maybe it's simply because I want it," he said. "Or perhaps you can find out the answer to that question for me between here and Sacramento."

"Are you planning the trip or am I?"

"I thought I'd book the two of you on a train—"

"How about if you leave that to me?" Clint suggested.

"What do you mean?"

"Give me some expense money and I'll plan the route."

"And you'll tell me about it."

"No."

Restin stopped drawing on his cigar. "Why not?"

"Because I still don't know what's really going on," Clint said. "I mean, that's the way I feel. So if you're trusting me to deliver your daughter to this college in Sacramento. I think you should trust me to plan the route."

"And not tell me what that route would be."

"And not tell anyone what the route is."

Now Restin drew on the cigar again blew out a plume of smoke.

"All right," he said, finally.

"You agree?"

"Yes."

"With what part?"

"All of it," Restin said. "I'll give you some expense money, and you plan the route."

"And the expense money doesn't come out of my fee."

"Of course not."

"Well, all right," Clint said.

"When do you want to start?" Restin asked.

"I need tomorrow to plan, and to finish up some other business."

"So day after tomorrow?"

"Bright and early in the morning," Clint said. "Have her mounted on a good horse."

"The best I've got," Restin said. "Don't worry, she'll be ready."

"Then I guess I'll be on my way," Clint said. "Thanks for the dinner."

"I'll have somebody get your horse," Restin said.

"Owens said he'd put him in the barn," Clint said. "I can get him."

"Very well," Restin said. "I'll see you day after to-morrow, early."

"I'll be up at first light," Clint said.

Restin nodded, and Clint went down the stairs and

headed for the barn.

He found Eclipse inside, fully saddled. When he mounted up and rode outside, Restin was still on the porch, smoking.

TWENTY-THREE

When he got to his hotel the desk clerk waved at him frantically. It was never an emergency with this man. Most of his movements were frantic.

"What is it?" Clint asked.

"I got some telegrams for you, Mr. Adams," the man said. "The clerk brought them in three separate times."

"Thanks," Clint said, accepting the telegrams. He took them to his hotel room to read them.

*****

The next morning he was able to make arrangements with the bank to pay the lawyer, Eugene Barkley, his fee. The other two telegrams he'd gotten were from two friends, Bat Masterson and the Denver private detective, Talbot Roper. Neither of them was available to help him deliver a girl to Sacramento. They apparently had some problems of their own to deal with.

Clint wasn't even sure he needed anyone to watch his back. But he still wasn't convinced that all Vance Restin was doing was hiring him to deliver his daughter to Sacramento. Something else had to be going on.

He decided to see how much more the sheriff knew, but he stopped for breakfast first.

As he walked into the café he spotted the sheriff sitting at a table.

"How'd you find me?" Moreland said, looking up as Clint approached.

"I didn't," Clint said. "You told me where you got my food while I was in your jail, and I thought I'd have breakfast here."

"Well, you're here," the lawman said. "Have a seat."

Clint sat. A waiter came over right away and he ordered steak and eggs, and coffee.

"I was going to stop by your office after I ate, though," Clint went on.

"What about?"

"I went out and had supper with the Restin family last night."

"That must have been fun," Moreland said. "Terry Restin as much of a handful as we've heard?"

"More."

"Did you take the job?"

"I took it."

"Good," Moreland said. "I didn't want to see any more of you in my jail."

The waiter brought Clint's steak and eggs.

"So tell me," the Sheriff said. "How do you intend to take her?"

"You mean what's my route going to be?"

"That's what I mean."

"I'm not saying."

"So you just told Restin?"

Clint shook his head while he chewed. "I'm not telling him, either."

"Well," Moreland said, "how did he take that?"

"He took it well," Clint said. "In fact, he gave me some travel money."

"Really?" The lawman looked surprised. "You got

money out of him?"

"Not much," Clint said. "But enough."

"Train? Stage?"

Clint didn't answer.

"What about taking a man with you?"

"For what?"

The sheriff shrugged. "To watch your back?"

Clint stopped eating and looked at the man. "You know, I thought about that, but...watch my back from what? What do you know?"

"Me? I don't know anything."

"A boyfriend? Is that what you're telling me?"

"I already told you, I don't know anythin' about that," Moreland said. "Look, I gotta get to work." He stood up. "Don't worry about paying for breakfast. It'll be on me."

"Thanks."

As the sheriff left, Clint still had half his breakfast remaining.

"Sir?" the waiter asked. "More coffee?"

"Yes, please," Clint said.

The waiter poured it and walked away.

Clint thought over the travel plans for himself and Terry the next day.

TWENTY-FOUR

Clint decided that a good portion of the trip to Sacramento—the first part, anyway—would be done on horseback. He wanted to check out Eclipse and make sure he was good for the trip.

He went to the livery and checked the horse's hooves and legs, walked him around a bit. The Darley Arabian was as sound as could be during the ride to and from the Restin ranch. This was really just a way to double check his soundness. And it was something for Clint to do while he worked the problem out in his mind.

The major question on his mind was, what was going on? Nobody pays that much money just to have somebody delivered to school. Clint decided that between here and Sacramento, he and Terry were going to get as lost as they could. No one was going to be able to track them, or find them, or guess what route they were taking.

Clint had hunted down many men in his time, but had not spent much time trying not to be tracked down by others himself.

This was going to be something new.

*****

"Come in and close the door," Restin said.

Dave Peterson entered the room and closed the door

behind him.

"Sit."

Peterson did. Maybe now he was going to find out when he could take care of Clint Adams.

"Is Terry in the house?" Restin asked.

"Yeah," Peterson said. "She's upstairs."

"Good, good."

"Mr. Restin," Peterson said, "what's goin' on? When do we get a chance at Adams?"

"Soon," Restin said, "very soon, Peterson. Where are your men?"

"In the bunkhouse," Peterson said, "makin' your men real uncomfortable."

"I'm going to need you to do something for me, Peterson," Restin said, "without question."

"No questions?" Peterson asked. "That ain't my way, Mr. Restin."

"But if I pay you enough it can be your way, right?" Restin asked.

"Well..." Peterson rubbed his jaw. "Totally without questions?"

"Absolutely."

"It would have to be a real good payday, Boss."

"Don't worry," Restin said. "It will."

*****

Later, Peterson entered the bunkhouse and told his men, "Outside."

"What for?" Stan Rhodes asked, looking at the full house he was holding.

"Just do it," Peterson said, "no questions asked."

He went outside and waited for his three men. His heart was racing. There was a lot of money at stake here, plus a chance at killing the Gunsmith.

The three men came out one at a time, tucking in their shirts, smoothing back their hair and putting their hats on, strapping on their guns.

"What's goin' on, Peterson?" Rhodes asked.

"I need you all to listen up," Peterson said.

The three men exchanged glances, but Rhodes was the spokesman.

"Yeah, okay."

"Let's get away from the bunkhouse," Peterson said. "I don't want the others to hear what I've got to say."

Hank Spenser, Ted Banks, and Stan Rhodes looked at each other, shrugged, and followed their boss.

Peterson led them around behind the barn, then turned to face them.

"Okay, Dave," Stan Rhodes said, "what's goin' on? I don't get it."

"The boss has just offered us a lot of money."

"We been gettin' a lot of money," Banks said.

"Yeah," Spenser said, "what's new about that?"

"Look," Peterson said, "I'm talkin' about a lot of goddamned money, not the chickenfeed we've been getting so far."

"Dave," Stan Rhodes said, "I was holdin' a full house in there—"

"Jesus Christ, don't you guys get it?" Peterson snapped. "We stand to make a fortune here."

"And what do we gotta do for it?" Spenser asked.

"You mean after we kill the Gunsmith?" Peterson asked. "Simple. The boss don't want his daughter to make it to that school in Sacramento—ever!"

TWENTY-FIVE

After Clint left Eclipse at the livery, satisfied as to the horse's perfect condition, he went to the Drinkwater for a beer. Buck was alone.

"Beer," Buck said, putting a frosty mug down in front of him.

"Thanks."

"When are you and the girl leavin'?"

Clint stared at the man.

"Ah, hell, don't tell me," Buck said, with a wave. "Just be careful."

"Of what?"

"Everythin'," Buck said. "Everybody."

"Buck," Clint said, "you hear everything that goes on in this place, don't you?"

"Pretty much."

"So you know things."

"I don't know nothin', Mr. Adams," Buck said. "Yeah, I hear some things, but I can't put them all together. I mean, not ever."

"You ever hear Restin talk about his daughter?"

"Sure," the bartender said. "He says he loves her and wants the best for her. To him that means sendin' her to school in Sacramento."

"Does he think somebody might be trying to keep her from getting there?"

"I don't think so," Buck said, "but then he's hirin' the Gunsmith to take her there, so what's that mean to you?"

"Something I don't like, Buck," Clint said. "Something I don't like."

*****

Clint went back to his hotel. As he entered, the clerk started waving again.

"You better calm down, friend," Clint said, approaching the desk. "You're going to give yourself a heart attack."

"Sorry, sir, but she's been sittin' there, waitin' for you for a couple of hours."

"She?"

The man inclined his head. Clint turned to look, expecting to see Beth. Instead, seated on a sofa in the lobby was Terry Restin.

*****

Vance Restin came charging out of his house, yelled out Ray Owens' name.

Owens came running out of the livery up to the house and stopped in front of his boss.

"What's the matter, Mr. Restin?"

"Have you seen Terry?"

"Ain't she in the house?"

"If she was in the house would I be asking you if you had seen her?"

"No, sir," Owens said, "I ain't seen her."

"Is her horse in the barn?"

"I, uh, didn't notice. I was lookin' in on that new foal—" the foreman tried to explain.

"Never mind that," Restin said, cutting him off. "Go

and check!"

"And if it's not there?"

"Then saddle mine," Restin instructed. "I have an idea where she might be."

"Yes, sir."

While Owens went back to the barn, Restin didn't wait. He went back into the house.

*****

"Terry," Clint said to her, "what are you doing here?"

"We need to talk."

"About what?"

"About what my father has hired you to do," she said. "Let's go to your room."

"Oh no," he said, "I'm not taking you to my room."

"Why not?"

"Because a Restin has already gotten me thrown into jail for something I didn't do."

She firmed her jaw and asked, "Do you really think I'd cry rape?"

"I don't know what you would or wouldn't do to avoid going to Sacramento," he told her. "If you really want to talk to me, let's go someplace else."

"The Drinkwater, then."

"I'm not taking you to a saloo—"

"Relax," she said. "My father owns it. I go there all the time. There's never anybody there."

"Well," he said, after a moment, "okay, but I'm not buying you a drink."

"Let's just go," she said. "I can buy my own damned drinks."

TWENTY-SIX

Clint walked Terry over to the Drinkwater Saloon, which he had only just left.

Actually, she stormed over there ahead of him and he had to hurry to catch up. She was a tall girl who took long strides when she was angry.

He entered the saloon behind her and she stalked over to the bartender.

"Give me a beer, Buck!" she demanded.

"Miss Restin," Buck said, "you know I can't do that. What would your father say?"

"Goddammit!" she swore. "Is every man in this town afraid of my father?"

"Buck works for your father, Terry," Clint said. "It's not fair of you to ask him to do something that will cost him his job."

She turned and looked at Clint. "Well, you're not afraid of him, I can tell that much," she said.

"No, I'm not."

"Then why are you working for him?"

"He's paying me five thousand dollars."

"Money means that much to you?" she asked. "It makes you work for a man you despise."

"And what makes you think I despise your father?" he asked her.

"I can tell."

"Terry," Clint said, "let's sit down. Buck, can we get two coffees?"

"That I can do," the bartender said.

They sat down at a table and Buck brought over two cups of coffee.

"Thanks," Clint said.

Buck gave him a look behind Terry's back and then returned to the bar.

"What's on your mind, Terry?"

"I want to buy you off, Clint," she said. "What'll it take? Money? My lily white body? I'm very good in bed. I may be young but I'm very experienced."

"I'm sure you are, Terry," Clint said, "but the answer is no on both counts."

"But why?"

"Can you keep my ass out of jail?" Clint asked. "Do you have any influence over the sheriff and the circuit judge? Can you keep me from being charged with—and tried for—shooting a man?"

She looked down at her cup and said, "No."

"Can you convince your father not to frame me for murder if I don't deliver you?"

"No."

"Then I think you better go on home and get yourself packed for the trip. And pack light. We're leaving on horseback."

"What? No stage? Or train?"

"We'll see, Terry," he said. "Go home."

She stood up, started away, then turned back.

"Go home! Pack!"

She turned and walked out the door.

"Beer?" Buck asked from the bar.

"Definitely."

Buck brought it over.

"You didn't have to worry about that little hellcat," the bartender said.

"Why's that?"

"I had my hand on my shotgun the whole time."

*****

Clint finished his beer and once again made the walk to his hotel. This time when he walked through the lobby the desk clerk averted his eyes.

Clint went up the steps and approached his room. When he got there the instincts that had kept him alive all these years kicked in. He placed the palm of his hand flat against the door and it was as if he could feel the presence of someone on the other side.

He drew his gun, slid the key into the lock, and swung the door open violently.

The girl on the bed jumped and held the sheet up to cover her nudity, and then realized it was him.

"Jesus, Clint!" she said. "You scared me half to death.'

"The desk clerk was acting funny."

"I paid him to let me in."

"I didn't know it was you, Beth," Clint said, grateful that he hadn't brought Terry up there with him.

"How did you know anyone was up here?"

"Like I told you, the clerk was acting funny," he said, "and I could feel that someone was here."

"Well," she said, "now that you know it's me could you put the gun away?"

He looked down at the gun in his hand, which was still pointing at her.

TWENTY-SEVEN

After he holstered the gun, then removed it and hung it within easy reach, she tossed the sheet away to reveal her nude body.

"Beth," he asked, "where does your family think you are this time?"

"Still working on that damned dress," she said. "I told them it's been givin' me starts and fits."

"And they believe you?"

"My family always believes what I tell them, Clint," she said.

"That's all well and good," he said, "but what are you doing here now?"

She pouted because she had reached for him and he'd stepped back.

"You're gonna be leavin' tomorrow, aren't you?" she asked.

"Well, yes, but—"

"Then this is the last chance I'll ever have to be with you."

"Beth—"

"After you leave I'll have to go back to my husband," she said. "Clint, he's so boring!"

"And your son?"

"Harry is wonderful, but this is not about him. This is about you and me."

"Beth—"She settled down on her back, raised one knee, put her hands behind her neck, and said, "Are you going to say no to this?"

Her nipples were already hard.

"You're the only man who makes me feel this way, Clint," she said, "wanton, and sexy. When you leave it will all be gone."

He stared at her naked body, then shook his head. There was no way to turn her down and still be human. He undid his belt and trousers and growled, "Damn you, woman!"

*****

As Terry was riding out of town she saw her father riding in.

"I thought I'd find you here."

"Daddy—"

"What were you trying to do?" he demanded. "Convince Adams not to take the job? Do you know what will happen to him if he doesn't?"

"Of course I do," she said. "He told me. Don't worry, he turned down everything I had to offer him—and I offered him everything."

"I don't want to hear that," Restin said. "Let's get back to the house."

"I know," Terry said. "I've got to pack!"

*****

Clint ran his finger along Beth's naked spine as she lay on her belly beside him.

"You have a beautiful back," he told her.

"You see?" she said. "That is something Ben would never say."

"You can't hold that against him, Beth."

She rolled over onto one elbow, so that her breasts were no longer crushed beneath her.

"Do me a favor, will you?" she asked.

"What's that?"

"Don't defend my husband to me while we're in bed together."

He sat up.

"I told you this was a bad idea," he said.

"Wait—"He stood up, grabbed his pants.

"I think you better go back to your family," he told her. "They're going to be looking for you."

"But Clint—"

"Come on," he said, sitting on the bed to pull on his boots. "I have to go and do something."

"A-all right," she said. She got off the bed and put her dress back on.

"What's so important?"

He didn't have anything to do, exactly, but he wanted her to go.

"I have to get ready to leave tomorrow."

"The word around town is that you're workin' for Vance Restin."

"That's the word?" he asked. "I'm doin' a job for him, under duress. That is not working for him."

"Taking his daughter to California?"

He stared at her.

"That's what they're saying around town?"

"You better watch out for Terry Restin, Clint," Beth warned.

Now he really did have something he had to do—find out who put the word out about him and Terry Restin.

"You'd better get home, Beth—" he said, moving to get off the bed, but she stopped him, using surprising strength to push him down on his back.

"Hey!" he said.

"Not so fast," she said. "Since you're gonna be out on the trail with that pretty young girl, I better give you somethin' to remember me by."

"What the—"She reached down to grasp his cock, began stroking it with one hand, while fondling his balls with the other.

"Beth—"

"Hush," she said. "Ben doesn't let me do this to him."

"Do wha—oh."

She slid down between his legs and began to lick his penis, from the base to the head, over and over again, until he was good and wet, and then she opened her mouth and took him inside.

"Jesus—" he said, lifting his butt off the bed.

She began to suck him, sliding her lips up and down the length of him, wetting him even more, so that her saliva ran down onto his testicles and thighs.

She sucked him avidly, moaning and even growling, inflaming him so much that it wasn't long before he was exploding into the hot depths of her mouth...

TWENTY-EIGHT

Clint let himself into the Sheriff's office without knocking, even though he really had no intention of going back there.

"Adams," Moreland said, looking up in surprise. "What's on your mind? You look...agitated."

"That's a good word for it."

"What is it?"

"I heard that the word has gone out around town about my little job for Restin."

"Oh, that."

"Yeah, that. Do you know who opened their big mouth about it? I assume it wasn't you."

Sheriff Moreland put his hands up and said, "I didn't say a word."

"Then who?"

"You got me," Moreland said. "Maybe you should just ask Restin."

"Restin! Why would he say a word?"

"I don't know," the lawman said. "Weren't you wonderin' why he hired you in the first place? So, why not ask another question?"

Clint shook his head. Restin would be crazy to say anything, but Clint still didn't know the whole story.

On the other hand, it could have been Terry Restin herself looking to make things difficult from the very beginning.

"But you know," Moreland said, "a ranch hand, a bartender, one of Restin's gunnies...all it would take is one."

"You're right about that."

"So calm down," the lawman suggested. "Just do the job and get it over with."

"Believe me," Clint said, "that's what I intend to do."

"Do you want me to ask around town and try to find out who talked?"

"No, just forget it." Clint replied. "I'll take care of it myself."

"Well, just do me a favor," the lawman said.

"What's that?"

"If you find out who did it, don't shoot anybody," Moreland said, "at least, not in town."

"Agreed," Clint said.

*****

Clint left the Sheriff's office, stopping just outside. The only thing left to do was buy some supplies for his trip with Terry Restin. Vance Restin's expense money was burning a hole in his pocket.

He went to the general store, bought some things that would fit easily into a burlap bag, which he would then hang from his saddle. He didn't want to take a pack animal along. It would only slow them down.

By the time he was done he had bought enough beef jerky, beans, bacon, cans of peaches, coffee, ammunition for both his weapons, as well as two new blankets that he knew he'd be hanging from Terry's saddle.

"Will you be takin' any of this with you now, sir?" the clerk asked.

"No," Clint said, "I'd like to pick it all up early tomorrow morning."

"Of course, sir," the man said. "And shall I put this on Mr. Restin's tab?"

"Why would you ask me that?"

"Uh, well, I just assumed, after what I've been hearin' around town--"

"And just exactly where did you hear what you heard?" Clint asked, cutting him off.

"Um, I don't rightly know, sir, just...around." The clerk looked nervous.

Clint said, "You know what? Go ahead and put this all on Mr. Restin's tab."

"All right, sir."

"And add some more of this...and this...and this..."

*****

Rhodes, Banks, and Spenser were in town, drinking in a saloon called the Black Queen.

"No matter what we told Dave Peterson," Rhodes said, "or what Dave told Restin, I ain't okay with this."

"I don't got a problem with it," Spenser said, "as long as we're gettin' paid as much money as Peterson said we was gonna."

"Oh, hey," Stan Rhodes said, "don't get me wrong. I didn't say I wasn't gonna go through with it, I just said I didn't like it."

"Hey!" Banks said. He was standing at the batwing doors, looking out over them. "Look who's here."

Rhodes and Spenser joined him at the door and looked out at Clint Adams, who was crossing the street. They watched as he strode on past.

"This would be real easy, now," Banks said. "All we

113

gotta do is step out--"

Rhodes put his hand on Banks' shoulder to stop him from saying more.

"I wanna kill him as much as you do," Rhodes said. "But not enough to mess up our chance at a lot of money first." He slapped Banks on the back. "Come back to the bar and drink your beer."

Rhodes walked back to the bar.

"He's right," Spenser said. "Come on."

He followed Rhodes back to the bar and, reluctantly, so did Banks.

*****

Clint left the general store after spending much more of Vance Restin's money than he'd intended to. As he crossed the street he pretended not to see three of Restin's hired guns watching him from the doorway of the Black Queen saloon.

He briefly considered going into the saloon and playing with the three men, because they must have been ordered not to brace him at any time—at least, until the job was over. But in the end he decided to stay away from them. After all, he'd promised the sheriff he wouldn't shoot anybody.

Not in town, anyway.

TWENTY-NINE

lint woke early the next morning, happy to be alone in his room. Beth was pleasant to be with, but he was tired—and a little ashamed—of violating Ben Ballard's marital bed. He felt badly about not saying goodbye to the boy, Harry, but felt it couldn't be avoided.

By the time he got Eclipse saddled and rode him over to the general store, the clerk had the supplies separated evenly into two burlap sacks—all except the two new blankets, which Clint tossed over Eclipse's back for the moment.

"Goin' out to Mr. Restin's ranch now?" the man asked, still nervous. As far as the man was concerned he was probably just another of Vance Restin's hired guns.

"As a matter of fact, I am."

"Would you, uh, please give him my, um, my best regards?"

"I'll do that."

Clint rode away. He didn't know the man's name, and hadn't bothered to ask.

*****

He rode up to the house and--true to his word—Vance Restin had his daughter's horse saddled and ready. His man, Ray Owens, was standing on the porch. When he saw Clint he came down to meet him, stopping to hold the horse's head. There was no sign of any of the ranch hands or gunnies.

As Clint dismounted, he grabbed one of the blankets and sacks from his saddle and carried them over to the girl's brown mare.

"Where is she?" he asked Owens.

"Inside. You want that stuff on the horse?"

"I do."

"I'll take care of it for you." Owens accepted the supplies from Clint. "You can go inside, if you want."

"I don't want," Clint said. "I told your boss to have her ready."

"She's ready."

"Then she should be out here."

Owens tied the sack and blanket to the girl's saddle and said, "I'll go in and tell them you're here."

"Tell them I won't be here in five minutes," Clint suggested.

Owens didn't know what to say to that, so he just nodded and went inside.

Clint looked around, couldn't detect anyone watching him—or holding a gun on him. When the front door opened he turned his attention back to it. Owens came out with Vance Restin, who was leading an obviously reluctant Terry Restin by the arm.

"I told you she'd be ready."

"Yeah," Clint said, "she looks ready."

"I'm ready to kill somebody!" she shouted.

"Well," Clint said, "don't make it me. I'm just the messenger."

"Get on the horse, Terry," Vance Restin said. "Ray, get her up on the horse."

She was wearing expensive riding clothes, right

down to the leather boots. Owens gave her a boost and she swung her leg over the saddle.

"You didn't have something a little more comfortable to wear?" Clint asked.

"These are my comfortable riding clothes, Mr. Adams!" she snapped.

"Well," he said, "we may have to stop and get you something else along the way."

"So now you propose to dress me as well as transport me against my will?"

"Whatever it takes, Miss Restin."

"Do I really need to have this hanging from my saddle?" she demanded, putting her hand on the burlap bag.

"Yes," he said, "you do. You need to carry your share of the supplies."

He turned and mounted Eclipse.

"Adams!" Restin said.

"Yes?"

The man handed Owens a piece of paper, motioned for him to give it to Clint.

"There's the address where to take her."

"Thanks." Clint took it and put it in his pocket.

"Aren't you going to read it?"

"Somewhere along the line I will," Clint said, "When I need to. Besides, I'm sure Terry knows where we're going."

"Terry does," she said, "but what makes you think I'd tell you?"

"We'll see," Clint said. He started to turn his horse.

"Don't you have something to say to me?" Vance Restin demanded.

"I do, actually," Clint said. "Somebody in your camp opened their big mouth about this job. You better find out who and do something about it. And if I find out there's something else going on here that I don't know about, and things go wrong, I'll be back for you."

"Is that a threat?"

"I don't make threats," Clint said, "I make promises—and I keep them."

Restin glared at Clint, but didn't say anything.

"Come on," Clint said to Terry.

As they rode through the front gate Terry said, "You left my father speechless."

"Good."

"Maybe you're not so bad after all."

"You think so?" Clint asked. "If I find out you're the one who opened her mouth about this job, I'm going to put you over my knee."

Terry just chuckled.

*****

After Clint Adams and Terry left, Vance Restin called Dave Peterson into his office.

"They're on their way," he said. "Are you and your men prepared to do what I asked you to do?"

"For half the money up front, we are."

Restin took a bulging envelope from his drawer and tossed it to the man, who caught it against his chest.

"Nobody but you and I know how much is in there," he said. "How much you want to pay your men is up to you."

"Understood."

"Just get the job done and the other half of the money is yours."

"Yes, sir."

"Then get to it!"

Peterson found his men outside the bunkhouse.

"What's goin' on?" Rhodes asked.

"Adams and the girl just left."

"And the money?"

Peterson took the bulging envelope and held it in his hand where they could see it.

"Paid in full," he lied.

"Jesus," Banks said, staring.

"Just like that?" Rhodes asked. "He paid us before the job?"

"It wasn't easy gettin' this out of him," Peterson said, "but I convinced him that we'd get the job done. Was I wrong?"

"Hell no!" Spenser said. "We'll do it."

Peterson looked at the other two, who both nodded.

"Then we better get outfitted. We don't know how long this will take."

THIRTY

Clint and Terry rode in utter silence for most of the first day. For Clint's part, he was paying special attention to their back trail. He just assumed that Terry wasn't talking because she wasn't happy.

But as dusk was approaching she turned in her saddle and asked, "So?"

"So what?"

"Are we being followed or not?" she said. "You've been looking behind us all day."

"Well," he said, "to tell you the truth, if someone was following us and knew what they were doing, I might not even see them. But for what it's worth, I don't think we're being tailed."

"And if we were?" she asked. "Why would anyone want to do that?"

"That's something I thought maybe you'd know better than I do."

"I haven't the faintest idea."

"You really don't know what your father is up to, Terry?"

"I'll tell you one thing, though," she said. "He's always up to something. He never does anything without a reason."

"That's what I'm worried about." He looked around. "We'll camp here."

121

"Thank God!" She dismounted and rubbed her bottom. "My ass is going to be sore for a week. Let me know when supper is ready. I'm going to sit—"

"You have two choices," he said, cutting her off.

"Do I?" she asked. "And what are they?"

"You can go out and collect wood and build a fire," he said. "Or you can take care of the horses."

"Take care of them?"

"Unsaddle them, rub them down, feed them, picket them—"

"Whoa," she said, "Horses get all that care?"

"They do," he said, "especially mine."

She sighed heavily.

"I guess I'll build a fire."

"Good." Clint said. "My horse probably would have bit your finger off."

She stared at him.

"Oh, and by the way," he said. "You can start cooking supper."

"Cook?" she said. "I don't cook."

"Then make beans," he said. "You can't ruin that. When I'm finished with the horses I'll make the coffee."

"And you're welcome to that job."

*****

By the time Clint finished with the horses Terry had somehow managed to make a fire. He had heard a lot of cussing coming from her, but there she was, with a pan of beans cooking over the fire.

"Nice job," he said.

"I'm burning them," she complained.

"Just move 'em around," he said. "You're doing fine."

He got the coffee pot, filled it with water, dropped coffee in, and set it down on the other side of the fire. Before long the air was filled with the smell.

"Here," Clint said, taking the pan from Terry, "you cooked, so I'll serve."

He spooned some beans into a plate, handed it to her with a fork, then poured a cup of coffee and handed it over. He served himself and began eating.

"Is this how you always eat out here?" she asked.

"Pretty much," he said. "I'll make supper tomorrow, and I'll add some bacon to the beans."

"You could have added some tonight."

"No, no," he said. "You were doing the cooking tonight."

She ate in silence for a while, then said, "Maybe tomorrow night you can show me what to do with the horses."

"I can do that."

"Without me losing any fingers?"

"We can definitely work on that."

*****

After supper he showed her how to clean the plates using dirt, and then she watched as he prepared another cup of coffee.

"I don't drink coffee much, but this strikes me as very strong."

"It is," he said. "It's trail coffee, but it's also the only way I drink it."

She drank some more and said, "I like it."

When they finished the coffee he said, "You better turn in now, We'll want to get an early start."

"Where are we going from here?"

"You'll find out tomorrow."

"You don't trust anyone, do you?"

"It's why I'm still alive."

"Are you going to sleep?"

"In a while."

"What are you going to do now?"

"I'm going to make sure we weren't followed."

"How?"

"While you sleep," he said, "I'm going for a stroll in the dark."

THIRTY-ONE

Clint waited until Terry's breathing was even, until he knew that she was asleep, before he melted into the darkness. He didn't really think they had been followed, but he was, in effect, dangling Terry as bait. He didn't go out strolling in the dark, as he had told her. Instead, he moved outside the ring of light thrown by the campfire, found a comfortable spot, and hunkered down to watch. He would probably do this for each and every night they were on the trail.

If anyone was going to come for them in the dark, he'd be ready.

On the other hand, if he was worrying for no reason, and no one was coming, at all, he'd be perfectly all right with that, too.

He remained hidden until the sun started to come up, then moved into camp and got a couple of hours sleep. He was awakened by the smell of coffee.

He rolled to his feet and saw Terry crouched by the fire, where a pot of coffee was boiling.

"I figured you were up late protecting me, so I decided to make the coffee."

"Thanks," he said, accepting a cup from her.

"But I didn't want to make beans for breakfast, and right now beans are all I can make."

"No problem," he said. "I'll make some pan biscuits

125

and bacon."

While he was preparing the biscuits she watched, shook her head, and asked, "Are you sure you're a gunfighter and not a cook?"

"I'm neither," Clint said.

"I didn't mean—you're a pretty touchy guy, aren't you?" she asked.

"I just don't like being labeled."

"You mean like you labeled me?"

"I never did that."

"You think I'm spoiled, a hellcat, a problem child," she said.

"I do think you're spoiled," he admitted. "I never said you were a hellcat."

When the bacon was cooked he took it out of the pan, then put the biscuits back into the bacon grease before serving it all.

"Well," she said, after tasting it, "I hope you can shoot as well as you cook."

"Hopefully, I won't have to—unless you know something I don't."

"There you go again," she said, "so suspicious."

"Until I see a reason <u>not</u> to be."

"And do you have reasons to <u>be</u> suspicious?" she asked.

"Life doesn't work that way," Clint said. "I need reasons not to be suspicious. That's just the way it is."

"Well, I guess I'm just not the one to give you that," she said.

"Maybe there is something you can help me with."

"Like what?"

"Like why you're so all fired against going to school in Sacramento."

"I'm not against going to school in Sacramento," she

said.

"Then what—"

"I just don't want to go to school."

"Why not?"

"Simple," she said. "Because my father wants me to."

"So you're just being difficult for the sake of being difficult. To annoy him?"

"Why else?" she asked. "Why would I be difficult for no good reason?"

"I can't say."

"Neither can I."

THIRTY-TWO

Rhodes, Spenser, and Banks were seated around the fire, drinking coffee and eating beef jerky for breakfast. Peterson allowed the coffee, but wouldn't relent on bacon or beans.

He was standing off to one side, staring ahead of them when Rhodes stood and took a cup of coffee to him.

"Thanks."

"What are you doin'?"

"Thinkin'."

"About what?"

"The when, the where," Peterson said.

"Why not how?"

"How would you do it?"

"Ride in on them and start shootin'." Rhodes said.

"Adams would never let you get close enough," Peterson said.

"Then what do you suggest?" Rhodes asked.

"That's what I'm thinkin' about," Peterson said. "Why don't you go back to the fire?"

Rhodes shrugged and walked away.

"What's goin' on with Dave?" Spenser asked.

"He says he's thinkin'."

"What about?"

"Adams and the girl."

"That boy thinks too much," Banks said. "Why don't

129

we just go—"

"I suggested that," Rhodes said, cutting him off. "He says Adams would never let us get close enough."

"He's right," Spenser said. "So leave the man alone and let him think."

"Why not?" Banks said with a shrug. "We got paid, and he's the boss."

Rhodes hunkered back down and poured himself another cup of coffee.

"I wouldn't be Peterson for nothing," Banks said.

"Why not?" Spenser asked. "He's smart."

"Like I said," Banks answered, "that boy thinks way too much."

"His head must hurt all the time," Spenser said.

The three men laughed.

Abruptly, Peterson came storming over to the fire and tossed the remnants of his coffee into the flames.

"You guys can stop laughing, break camp, and get mounted up."

"You decide how you wanna play this, Dave?" Rhodes asked.

"I have," Peterson said. "You three are gonna ride up ahead of them."

"And what are you gonna do?"

"I'll tell you about it as we saddle the horses..."

THIRTY-THREE

lint and Terry rode for two more days. The second night he showed her how to take care of the horses, and the third night she took care of them herself.

"More coffee?" she asked.

"Sure."

She reached across the fire and poured it for him, even though he had prepared the pot and the meal.

She was right about him, he was suspicious about people, and right now he was suspicious of her. Why was she being so nice and cooperative?

"You're doing it again," Terry said.

"What?"

"You're wondering what I'm up to," she answered. "What am I up to, what is my father up to...why don't you just rest your brain?"

Clint leaned forward.

"I know your father is up to something, Terry," he said. "You know it, too. You said as much. I just need to be ready for whatever it is. I'm not going to let him railroad me into a cell again."

"And me?"

"You're harder to read. But you've been very cooperative these past few days. Can you see how that would look suspicious to me?"

She stared at him.

"Come on," he chided, "a few days ago could you see yourself unsaddling horses and making beans?"

"No," she admitted. "But that doesn't mean I'm up to something." She stood up, walked around the fire to his side. "If I was up to something maybe I'd so something ... like this."

She stood behind him, pressed up against him, and put her hands on his shoulders. Even after days on the trail she smelled good.

"Terry—"

"Or this?" She leaned over, pressed her breasts against the back of his neck, and ran her hands down over his chest.

"Terry, come on..."

"Or this?" She moved one of her hands to cup his chin, lifted her head, and kissed him. Her mouth was hot and avid on his. They kissed for a long time, and then she slid into his lap and kissed him even harder.

She pulled her mouth away from his and said breathlessly, "Isn't this suspicious behavior?"

"Yes."

"Do you want me to stop?"

"No."

They kissed again...

After a while they moved away from the fire and spread out their blankets on the ground. Clint wasn't being a fool. Even if Terry was trying to pull something he was taking her up on her generous offer to sample her wares. After all she was a lovely girl with smooth skin and firm breasts.

Undressed they sank down to the blankets in a hot embrace. Clint, however, still had the presence of mind to make sure his gun was within easy reach.

He kissed her breasts, sucked her nipples, and slid

one hand down between her legs. She gasped as his fingertip found her wetness.

"Oh God," she said as a shudder passed through her body.

He didn't know how experienced she was. After all, she was very young. He was breaking a lot of his unwritten rules lately—no sex with married women, no sex with very young women. But this young woman needed to be kept busy so that no trickery could occur to her, and this was a very pleasant way to do it.

He kissed his way down her body and she looked down at him as he nestled his face between her legs.

"W-what are you doing?" she asked.

"Relax," he said, "you'll like it."

"But...nobody's ever done that be—ohhh." She reached down to grab his head as his tongue began to work on her.

Initially, he thought she was going to try to pull his head away, but in the end she simply held it in her hands, and then applied pressure to keep him there.

He moved his hands over her body, rubbing her breasts, pinching her nipples, so she'd have a variety of sensations to contend with. Finally, her entire body was wracked by spasms and he realized she'd just had an experience she'd never had before.

As he got to his knees she folded herself into a fetal position and laid there, catching her breath.

"You..." she said, then tried again. "You...what was that? I've never...felt anything like that before?"

"That's probably because up until now you've only been with boys, fumbling around in barns."

"Does that...is that what's supposed to happen... every time?"

"With the right person."

She looked at him, stretched her body out again, and asked. "Now what?"

"You want more?"

"Don't you?"

"I haven't even got started yet."

THIRTY-FOUR

lint was sure that Terry thought she was seducing him. He didn't know what she had in mind beyond that, but thought he had pretty much turned the tables on her.

They slept in each other's arms, but she was so exhausted from the night's activities that he was able to slip from her grasp, stoke the fire, and make coffee. The smell woke her up.

He was pouring two cups when he heard something.

"What a night—" she started, but he silenced her with a swipe of his hand.

Eclipse was also showing agitated signs of having heard something.

"What is it?" she asked, keeping her voice down.

"Somebody's out there."

She turned to look. "Where?"

"I don't know for sure," he said. "Just out there... somewhere."

"What do we do?"

"Hunker down," he said. "Stay down low, no matter what happens."

"What's going to happen?"

"Get down!" he said. "They're coming in now."

They both listened intently, hearing someone approaching. It took a while. Finally, a man on horseback appeared, entering their camp.

Clint recognized him.

"That's Dave Peterson," Terry said. "He works for my father."

"I know."

"Be careful," she warned. "He wouldn't come alone."

"Just stay down."

Clint took a few steps forward, positioned himself between the rider and the girl, and waited.

Peterson rode up and stopped about ten feet away.

"Adams."

"Peterson."

"You know my name."

"Terry knows it," Clint told him. "I don't know you from Adam."

Peterson grinned as if it was a joke, then realized it was not.

"What do you want here?" he asked.

"The girl, actually."

"Why?"

"I'll tell her."

Clint moved aside just enough for the hired gun to see Terry.

"Miss Restin," Peterson said, "your father has sent me to bring you home."

"And what happens to my original deal with Mr. Restin?" Clint asked.

"Mr. Restin says he released you from that deal," Peterson said.

"And he doesn't want me back in Festus?"

"He doesn't care where you go."

"Don't believe him, Clint," Terry said. "That doesn't sound like my father."

"Miss Restin," Peterson said, "you really should

saddle your horse and come home with me. Your father is waiting for you."

"And what about going to school in Sacramento?" she asked.

"He doesn't care about that," the gunman said. "He just wants you back."

Terry, hunkered down by the fire all this time according to Clint's instructions, suddenly stood up and said very loudly, "No."

"What?"

"No," she repeated. "I'm not going with you. I'm staying with Clint."

"But Miss-"

"You heard what she said, Peterson," Clint said. "This play isn't working for you, so you better just go ahead make your next one."

"What next one?"

"Tell your boys to come on in."

"You think I need help taking care of you, Adams?" Peterson asked.

"I've known men like you my whole life, Peterson," Clint said.

"And what kind of men are those, Adams?"

"Your kind run in packs," Clint said. "You don't have the nerve to face anybody man-to-man, one against one, on your own—let alone me."

"That's what you think?"

Clint laughed.

"That's what I know, Peterson," he said. "Why don't you step down from your horse and prove me wrong?"

"You know what, Adams?" Peterson said. "That's exactly what I'm gonna do."

"Clint—"

"I know, Terry," Clint said. "Just move aside, out of the line of fire."

THIRTY-FIVE

Rhodes, Spenser, and Banks had succeeded in circling to the east and then working their way back until they were ahead of Clint Adams and Terry Restin.

"How do we know we're in time?" Spenser asked.

"Yeah," Banks said, "what if Peterson's already dead?"

"Either of you hear a shot?"

"No," Spenser said.

"Nuh-uh," Banks said, shaking his head.

"Then he's not dead."

"Yeah, but still—" Spenser said.

"Peterson and me checked our watches," Rhodes said. "Don't worry, we're right where we're supposed to be."

"So what do we do now?" Banks asked.

"We dismount and move in closer."

"How do we know they even camped for the night?" Spenser asked.

"Why wouldn't they?"

"Some people travel at night," Banks said.

"When they have a reason to," Rhodes said. "Look, this was the point of us getting in front of Adams, to catch him while he was camped. Now I saw his fire last night, so I know he's camped."

"And what's Peterson doin'?" Banks asked.

"He's movin' in the front."

"When?"

Rhodes took out his watch, looked at it and said, "Right about now! And if we don't move, we're liable to hear some shots."

"Why didn't Peterson tell all of us this plan instead of just you?"

"Because neither of you would have remembered it, would you?"

Banks and Spenser looked at each other.

"Come on," Rhodes said, "we have to move in until we hear voices..."

*****

Peterson watched as Terry moved away, out of the line of fire.

"Well?" Clint said. "Either dismount or turn your horse around."

Peterson didn't move. That's when Clint realized he was waiting for something.

Or someone.

Or three someones.

Clint listened intently. This could be tricky.

*****

Peterson was waiting, hoping that Stan Rhodes was able to get those other two idiots, Banks and Spenser, into position. Without them this plan could go terribly wrong.

Of course, that all depended on how fast the Gunsmith was now that he was older than he used to be—and whether or not Peterson was as fast as he thought he was.

He had told Vance Restin that he could outdraw Clint

Adams. He had assured his boss of that, without a doubt. He still thought he could, and Restin had told him to take care of things in a way that was sure to work—and this was it.

But Dave Peterson still wanted to do it his way. He only wished he had some witnesses. Of course, the girl would see him gun down the Gunsmith, but she wouldn't live much longer after that herself.

"You going to dismount or turn and run, Peterson?" Clint Adams asked.

"I'm dismounting, Adams," he said.

*****

Rhodes held his hand up, stopping Spenser and Banks behind him.

"What?" Banks asked.

"Shh," Rhodes said. "Listen."

They all listened, and they heard voices.

"That's them," Rhodes said. "Okay, spread out."

*****

Clint watched, listened, and waited. He had to split his senses if he and Terry were going to come out of this alive.

Peterson slid his foot out of his stirrup, brought his leg around to dismount. As he did, he drew his gun, hoping to catch Clint flatfooted.

It didn't work.

Clint saw exactly what the man was doing. He drew his own gun and fired. The bullet struck Peterson solidly, yanked him right from the saddle. As he hit the ground with a thud his gun went flying.

"Jesus!" Terry gasped. "Clint—"Clint looked at her,

141

held his left hand out for her to stay put. He walked to the fallen man and checked him.

"Is he dead?"

"He is," he said. "But his partners are here."

"Where?"

At that moment someone stepped on a twig and it snapped, sounding like a stick of dynamite.

"There!" he said.

THIRTY-SIX

lint quickly rushed to Terry's side and crouched down next to her.

"Where are they?" she asked.

"They'll be coming in," he explained, "now that they heard a shot."

"B-but...from where?" she asked. "Where will they come from?"

"There's three of them," he explained, "so they'll come from three sides."

Her head swiveled around as she tried to look at all sides at once. "All at once?"

"Yes."

"But...there's only one of you."

"That's what they're counting on."

"Well...give me a gun."

"What?"

"I can help," she said. "Without a gun, I'm in the way. With a gun, I can help."

He moved quickly to his saddle and saddlebags, grabbed his rifle, and skittered back to her.

"Can you shoot a rifle?"

"Of course."

As he handed it to her, they came...

*****

143

Spenser moved first. He saw Peterson lying on the ground. The man had the money on him, that's what he was worried about.

"Damn it!" he swore, and broke into the open, hoping to get to Peterson's body. . .

Banks was thinking the same way. Peterson was down, probably dead, and all the money was with him. Or did Adams take it off him already?

He saw Spenser make his move and started running himself, his gun held out in front of him...

Rhodes saw that Peterson was down, and knew he had to take over, be the new leader. That meant he had to get that money from Peterson—or from Adams.

Spenser moved first, and then he saw Banks go. He gripped his gun tightly, and followed.

*****

"Protect yourself!" Clint said to Terry. "Don't try to help me, but protect yourself."

He stood, gun in hand, saw the men coming, one, two, and then three.

Two of the men were running to Peterson's body. The third man stopped in his tracks, looked at Clint, and raised his gun.

"Don't do it!" Clint called.

The man didn't listen. He fired a wild shot, missed, then prepared to fire a more well aimed shot.

Clint couldn't wait. He fired...

*****

Rhodes felt the bullet strike him squarely in the chest. The air went out of his lungs, the strength faded from his hands. He dropped his gun to the ground, and then fell on top of it.

Clint took in the action in an instant, saw that the other two men were running toward the fallen Peterson. He decided to hold off on any more shooting and see what they had planned.

THIRTY-SEVEN

Spenser and Banks reached the fallen Dave Peterson at the same time. They started going through his pockets, and it was Spenser who came out with the envelope stuffed with money.

"Gimme that!" Banks snapped.

"Later!" Spenser said. "Here comes Adams!"

They both turned as Clint advanced on them. His gun was back in his holster.

"You boys find what you wanted?"

The two men faced him, guns in hand. And in his left hand, Spenser had the envelope filled with money. There was no way in hell he was going to let that go.

"Adams," Banks said. "We don't want no trouble. You killed Peterson and Rhodes. That's enough for us. We'll just mount up and be on our way."

"Yeah," Spenser said. "How about it?"

Before any of them could speak they all heard the lever on a rifle being worked.

"Leave the money," she said.

"What?" Spenser asked.

Clint turned his head just slightly, to see Terry Restin standing right next to him, her rifle trained on the two paid gunmen.

"The money my father paid you," she said. "You can both ride out, but you have to leave the money right there

147

on the ground."

"Now look, girlie," Banks said, almost panicking at the thought of leaving the money behind, "we earned all of that money—"

"Oh yeah?" Clint asked. "And just how do you think you did that?"

Neither man commented.

"So, what exactly was your job?" Clint asked. "What were you going to do to this girl after you bushwacked and killed me?"

"Look, Adams—"

"What was it?" Clint asked, cutting Banks off. "Rape? Murder?"

"Naw, naw," Spenser said, "it wasn't nothin' like that. Honest."

"Then what?" Clint asked. "Come on, give it to us. You've got two choices. Tell us what we want to know or use those guns."

Spenser's left hand tightened on the envelope. He didn't want to give it up. "You need this little girl to back your play, Adams?" he asked, deciding on another tactic. "That ain't what I heard about the Gunsmith."

"It doesn't really matter to me what you think you've heard about me," Clint said. "I think I might just step aside and let this little girl take matters into her own hands. What do you think of that?"

Banks laughed shortly. "That'd be givin' her old man just what he paid us for."

Spenser gave his partner a dirty look, but it was too late to take the remark back.

"And what does that mean?" Clint asked. "Wait, are you trying to say her father hired the four of you to kill me, and then her?"

The two men looked at each other, and then at the

148

girl with the rifle.

"You're bluffin'," Banks said.

"You're right," Clint said. "I am bluffing."

The two men looked smug, but only for a moment.

"I would never have her do something I could do my-self," Clint went on. "Now what's it going to be? Your partners are starting to rot. We've got to get them buried. Are you going to walk away or be buried with them?"

Banks looked over at the two bodies, but Spenser looked at the money in his hand.

"Okay," he said, "okay, tell the girl to put the rifle down."

"Go on, Terry."

"But—"

"Put it down and go sit by the fire."

"Clint—"

"Do as I say."

Reluctantly, the girl lowered the rifle and walked back to the fire. Clint turned his head just slightly to make sure she went.

Spenser held his left hand out a bit so that Banks could see the money in it and raised his eyebrows. Banks nodded, and they both started to bring up their guns.

"Clin—" Terry started to shout, but she realized that Clint knew what was happening all along. As she watched, he drew his gun quicker than her eyes could follow and shot both men, who already had their guns in their hands.

The two men fell over backwards, their guns falling from their lifeless hands. However, Spenser's left hand closed tightly around the envelope of money.

Terry ran to Clint's side.

"You knew," she said.

"They had to try it," Clint said. "It was all about that

money."

Terry stepped forward, reached down carefully to grab the envelope in Spenser's hand without actually touching the dead man. She had to pull very hard to free it from his death grip.

"We'll take that money back to your father," Clint said to her.

"Why the hell would we do that?" Terry asked. "This is yours."

"I don't want it."

"Why not?" she asked. "You earned it."

"That's blood money," Clint said. "You keep it if you want to."

"You bet I will," she said. "What do we do now?"

"First," he said, "I bury these men."

"Why?" she demanded. "They tried to kill us."

"They're men," Clint said. "They have a right to a decent burial. I'll handle it myself."

"I can help..." she said, reluctantly.

"That's okay," he said. "You pulled that money from a dead man's hand. You've had enough contact with them. Why don't you put on a fresh pot of coffee?"

"Are you going to dig four graves?" she asked.

"No," he said, "one shallow grave for the four of them, just so their bodies aren't fed on. They deserve a decent burial, but not that decent."

THIRTY-EIGHT

When Clint came back from burying the four men he found that Terry had made a fresh pot of coffee and some bacon.

"I didn't know," she said, "if you wanted to eat anything after killing four men. I mean, I-I didn't know if you <u>could</u> eat—"

"One has nothing to do with the other," he said, and added to himself, *anymore*. There was a time when he couldn't eat after having to kill a man, but that was a long time ago. The truth of the matter was, he was hungry.

They sat around the fire, drank coffee, ate bacon, and talked.

"What do we do now?" she asked.

"Do you believe that your father sent those men to kill us?" he asked. "To kill <u>you</u>?"

She thought a moment, then said, "I wouldn't put anything past my father, but I can't imagine he has any reason to want me killed."

"But?"

"But where else would they have gotten that much money?" she asked.

"So you do believe it."

She hesitated, then said. "Yes."

"Do you love your father?"

"No." This time she answered without hesitation.

151

"Do you think he loves you?"

"No," she said. "I think he thinks he owns me."

"So he can do anything he wants with what he owns, right?" Clint asked.

"That's the way he thinks."

Clint drank coffee, munched on some bacon.

"I think," he said, finally, "we're going back."

"But he has other gunmen," she said. "And he wants to kill me for some reason."

"Do you want to find out why?"

"Well, yes, but...I don't want to get killed while I'm doing it."

"I won't let you get killed."

"And I don't want you to get killed."

"Well," he said, "I definitely won't let that happen."

"What was your plan for taking me to Sacramento?" she asked.

"I had a variety of thoughts on that," he said. "Part of the way on horseback, part on stage, the rest by train, but now I don't think you should go at all."

"Well," she said, "I never wanted to go in the first place."

"Okay," he said, "we have to be totally together on this, Terry."

"I--I don't know what you mean," she said. "We are together."

"Are we?" he asked.

"Clint," she said, "you're confusing me."

"I've been pretty confused this whole time, Terry," he said. "Confused by your father, and confused by you. I get the feeling I'm a pawn in a game the two of you are playing. Maybe some kind of power play?"

"How could I make a power play against him?"

"I don't know, Terry," Clint said. "I'm asking...do I

know everything?"

She bit her lip and looked away. He thought he saw a tear in her eye, but she blinked quickly.

Finally, she looked at him again.

"He killed my mother."

"How?"

"He beat her into the ground," she said. "I don't mean physically. He broke her spirit, broke her heart."

"Tell me."

"First," she said, "do we have anything stronger than coffee..."

Clint took a bottle of whiskey out of his saddlebags. It wasn't really for drinking, but for wounds. He poured some into her coffee cup and handed it to her, didn't have any himself.

"Go on."

"Nothing much more to tell," she said. "I was five, watched him berate her, humiliate her. I watched her cry. She loved me, but in the end she couldn't take it anymore. She went to the barn and hung herself."

"Terry, are you sure—"

"I found her."

"Okay, but someone else could have hung her up—"

"I didn't just find her," Terry went on. "I walked into the barn just as she threw herself off the hay loft. I heard her neck break."

"Jesus..."

"I blame him," she said. "I always have."

"And what about him?" Clint asked. "Who did he blame?"

"He never took an ounce of responsibility."

"Did he blame you?"

"Who knows?" she said. "He raised me after that, but he never showed me any love."

Clint ate his last piece of bacon, washed it down with the last of the coffee.

"I guess it's not much of a leap from not loving someone to having them killed, then," he said. "But still...what would be the reason to kill you now?"

"I don't know."

"How old are you?"

"I just turned twenty one."

He rubbed his jaw.

"That might have something to do with it."

"What do you mean?"

"Tell me, how did your father make his money?"

"Most of it came from my mother's family."

"So the money was hers."

"Yes."

"And when she died," he asked, "do you know what the will said?"

"No," she said, "I never saw it."

"Well," he said, "then we have a place to start."

"What do you mean?"

He stood up.

"Let's break camp and head back to Festus," he said. "We're going to get a look at that will."

THIRTY-NINE

ance Restin was impatiently waiting in the Drinkwater Saloon when his foreman, Ray Owens, came in.

"Any word?" Restin asked.

"No," Owens said, "none."

Restin slammed his fist down on the table.

"Peterson was supposed to send word when it was done!" he growled.

"Mr. Restin, the Gunsmith may have just killed them all," Owens said.

"There were four of them!"

"I know, sir, but...he is the Gunsmith."

Restin poured himself a glass of whiskey and downed it, never offering his foreman a drink.

"Ray," he said, "you have to find me more gunmen."

"But why?" Owens asked. "If Adams gets Terry to Sacramento—"

"If Adams killed them," Restin said, "then he knows they came after him on my orders."

"How could he know that?"

"One, he's not an idiot," Restin said, "and two, one of them might have told him before they died. If so, he's coming back here. And if he's doing that, I need more men." He glared at Owens. "And why am I explaining this all to you? Get out and get me some more men!"

"Yeah, sure, Boss," Owens said, and left the saloon.

155

*****

It was only about ten minutes later when the sheriff came walking in.

"What do you want?" Restin asked without giving the man a chance to speak.

Unlike Owens, Sheriff Moreland pulled out a chair and sat down.

"I don't want you to make a big mistake, Vance."

"When have I ever made a mistake, Moreland?" Restin asked. "And when have I ever needed your advice about anything?"

Moreland shrugged and said, "Well, maybe startin' now."

Buck came walking over with a cold beer and started to set it down.

"Don't give the sheriff a beer," Restin said. "He's just leaving."

Moreland stood up and grabbed the beer from Buck before he could retreat. He sipped it, then handed it to the bartender.

"Now I'm leavin'," he said.

*****

Restin entered his house and shouted, "Everett!"

His houseman came running out. "Sir?"

"I want you to start wearing a gun."

"A gun?"

"Yes."

"When?"

"All the time."

The man stared at him. He was in his fifties, and guns were a thing of his past.

"I know, I know," Restin said, "that's not why I hired

you, but—"

"Is this about Clint Adams?"

"It is."

"Is he coming back?"

"Probably."

"And Mr. Peterson and his men?"

"They probably aren't coming back."

"I see."

"Everett," Restin said, "I hate to ask this of you—"

"Forget it," Everett said. "It's been a while since I strapped on a gun, but I think I can find one."

"Good," Restin said, "because I'm going to start wearing one in the house, too."

"And will you be replacing Mr. Peterson and his men?"

"As soon as I can."

"Right."

"I'll be in my office," Restin said. "If Ray comes, send him in. And if anybody brings a telegram—"

"--I'll bring it right to you."

"Thank you."

"Sir."

Restin walked down the hall to his office.

*****

Mike Everett went to his own room, to a chest he kept in a corner. Inside the chest were the items he held most important in his life. He opened the chest, dug down beneath some clothes, an old bedroll and blanket, saddlebags, and came up with something wrapped in cloth. He unwrapped it and held it in his hand. The gun felt right, even though he hadn't held it in years.

He reached further down, came up with a leather

shoulder rig and holster that had been made especially for this gun. When he strapped it on he stretched his arms out. The rig felt comfortable, natural, made him wonder why he had ever taken it off.

He put a jacket on over the rig, left his room to go back to work.

FORTY

Clint and Terry had been riding for about three days when Peterson and his men caught up to them, but it took only two days for them to get back.

On the outskirts of Festus, Clint reined Eclipse in, and Terry followed his example with her mare.

"Now what?" she asked.

"I don't want your father to know we're here," he said, "even though I think he knows we're coming."

"How would he know that?"

"He's sure to have made arrangements with Peterson to notify him when the job was done," Clint said. "When he doesn't hear from him after a few days, he'll figure he and his men are dead."

"So?"

"Once he thinks they failed and that I killed them, he'll be waiting for me to come back for him."

"But he has plenty of men."

"And he'll probably hire some more to replace Peterson and his crew," Clint said.

"So what do you want to do? Go to the ranch?"

"No," Clint said, "that'd be riding into the lion's den. I'm sure he's got men watching for me."

"What about me?" she asked.

"What do you mean?"

"I could ride into the ranch," she said. "Nobody's

159

going to stop me."

"Terry, your father's already tried to have you killed once," Clint reminded her.

"I know that, Clint," she said, "but would he kill me right there at the ranch? If so, why didn't he just do it before? Why send me to Sacramento to have me killed on the trail? Because he won't do it at home."

"Maybe."

"I could ride in and tell him that you're coming for him," she said. "That would scare him."

"Wait," he said, "let me think about this. Maybe there's another message I could send him."

"Like what?"

"I don't know," he said. "Look, we need a place to hole up. Any ideas?"

"Actually, yes," she said, smiling, "I do have one idea. Follow me."

*****

When Ray Owens knocked on Restin's door the rancher looked up and snapped, "Well, come on in. Are you waiting for a special invitation?"

"Uh, no, Boss."

"What've you got?"

"I hired half a dozen guns," Owens said.

"Are they good?"

"Best I could find in town," Owens said. "Do we have time for me to look out of town?"

"I don't know," Restin said. "Send some telegrams and see what you can find."

"Yes, sir. Uh, do you want to meet the new men?"

"No, I don't want to meet them," Restin said, "I just want them to keep me alive. Position them around the house."

"Yessir."

"And set up a watch. I want the road observed at all times."

"Yessir."

"And the back trail."

"Yessir."

"So get out and get it done!"

"Right, Boss."

As Owens left, Restin sat back in his chair and rubbed his face vigorously with both hands. Things were not going according to plan at all.

*****

Terry took Clint to a house standing alone in a meadow—or barely standing. It was obvious no one had lived there for a long time, and it was on the verge of falling down.

"What's this place?" he asked.

"This is the house I was born in."

Clint didn't know what to say to that.

"My father would never dream of coming here," she said. "He hates it. It reminds him that he had no money and had to depend on my mother's in the beginning."

They dismounted in front of the house. Close up it seemed a bit sturdier than Clint had first thought.

"Don't worry," she said, "it won't cave in on us."

They went through the front door and entered the dusty interior. There was no furniture, but they'd be able to put their bedrolls down with no problem.

"Okay," he said, "this will do for a while."

"What do you mean for a while?" she asked.

"Couple of days, maybe."

"Why that long?"

"Your father's going to be waiting for us to come back," Clint said. "I'm thinking we let him wait a while longer, let him get nervous."

"But in the end," she asked, "how will you get to him?"

"I think," Clint said, "we'll have to get him to come to us."

FORTY-ONE

They built a fire inside the house, in the center of the floor, after Clint took the horses around back. Clint prepared coffee, bacon, and beans and they sat on the floor and ate.

"How many nights are we going to spend here?" she asked.

"I'm not sure," he said. "One or two. After we eat I'm going to slip into town to see the sheriff."

"Do you trust him?" she asked. "I'm sure he works for my father."

"Well, if I was going to trust anyone it would be the lawman in town," Clint said. "Do you have a better idea?"

"What do you want to do?"

"I need to talk to someone who knows something about your father," Clint said. "Maybe they can help me lure him away from his house and his men."

"I wouldn't trust the sheriff."

"Who, then?"

"Buck."

"The bartender at the Drinkwater?"

"Yes."

"Why would I trust him? He works for your father, too."

"Not because he wants to," she said. "Buck used to

163

own the Drinkwater. My father made him sell, then kept him on as a bartender. Buck doesn't like my father. If you can trust anyone in town, it's Buck."

"All right, then," he said. "I'll talk to Buck."

*****

After they finished eating she went out back with him and watched while he mounted Eclipse.

"What am I supposed to do in the meantime?" she asked.

"Stay here," he said. "Don't leave. I'll bring some real food when I come back."

"And what if someone comes along?"

He reached into his saddlebag, came out with the little Colt New Line he used as a hideout gun.

"Take this and use it if you have to," he said.

She accepted the gun. He remembered how her hands were shaking when she held the rifle on the two gunmen. He had no idea if she would have been able to shoot them or not.

"Terry," he asked, "have you ever shot anyone?"

She hesitated, then said, "No...but there's always a first time, right?"

He nodded, picked up Eclipse's reins.

"Be careful," she said, "and don't forget that real food."

"I'll be back soon," he promised.

She watched him ride off, then went back into the little house where she had been born.

*****

Clint knew there was little chance of riding into town on Eclipse and going unnoticed. Instead, he dismounted

164

several hundred yards away and walked the horse into town, but stayed off the main streets. Eventually, he found his way to the back door of the Drinkwater Saloon.

"Just stay right here, fella," he said to Eclipse, dropping the horse's reins to the ground. "I'll be right back."

He tried the back door, found it locked. He tried to force it, but it was solid. He'd have to go in the front.

Using the alley alongside the building he made his way to the front. Peering out, he waited until he was fairly sure he wouldn't be seen, then moved quickly to the batwing doors. One glance told him the place was empty, and he slipped inside.

The bartender looked up from the bar and regarded Clint quizzically as he approached.

"I thought you were gone," the man said.

"I was," Clint said. "I'm back now."

"So soon? Where'd you drop Terry off?"

"I didn't," Clint said. "Her father sent Peterson and his three partners to kill me...and her."

"What?"

"Can we lock the doors?"

"Sure."

Buck came around the bar, walked to the door closed them and locked them, then went back around behind the bar.

"Beer?" he asked.

"Yeah, thanks."

Buck set a cold mug in front of him.

"Still got that shotgun under the bar?"

"Yeah," Buck said. "You want it?"

"No," Clint said. "Terry says if I have to trust anybody in town, it should be you."

"That's probably because she knows I don't like her father," Buck said. "What do you need? And what do you mean he tried to have her killed? His own daughter?"

"Yes."

"Jesus," Buck said. "That's sick."

"You have any idea why he'd want to do that?"

"Me? No," Buck said. "I don't know the guy. I just know I don't like him."

"So you don't know anything about his will, then?" Clint asked.

"No."

"Never heard him talk about it in here?"

"Maybe," Buck said, "but nothing specific. Why?"

"I'm thinking the only reason he'd want to kill his daughter must have something to do with his will. Or his wife's will."

"His wife?" Buck asked. "She died when Terry was little."

"I know," Clint said. "Five."

"What do you want from me?" Buck asked.

"I might need to get him away from his ranch," Clint said, "away from his men."

"He always has men with him. Maybe more now that you killed Peterson and the others. Does he know that, by the way?"

"He's probably guessed by now. How often does he come here?"

"A few times a week."

"To see how the business is going?"

"What business?" Buck asked. "Nobody comes here, and that's the way he likes it. This place is just for him."

"To drink?"

"To drink and do business."

"But you don't know anything about his business."

Buck shook his head. "I hear things, but I don't understand them."

166

"What if you sent him a message that you had to see him?" Clint asked. "Would he come?"

Buck shrugged. "I don't know. I've never tried it."

"Would you be willing to do it?"

"I suppose," Buck said, "if it would help you. But... isn't it the wills you want to see? His and his wife's?"

"Yes, but he'd never—"

"Why don't you go and see his lawyer?"

"I don't know—do you know who his lawyer is?"

"I do know that much," Buck said. "It used to be old Mr. Henderson, bur he died a few years back."

"Did someone take over his practice?" Clint asked.

"Not really," Buck said. "He was an old man, his practice had fallen off. Restin was one of his last clients."

"So what did Restin do? Get a lawyer from somewhere like San Francisco?"

"No," Buck said, "he hired a new lawyer right here in town."

"Well, that's good," Clint said. "I just need to go to that lawyer and get a look at Terry's mother's will."

"You think he'll show it to you?"

"I don't think I'll give him a choice," Clint said. "All I need from you is his name."

"Sure, I understood that much," Buck said. "The lawyer's name is Eugene Barkley."

FORTY-TWO

Eugene Barkley.

Why did that not surprise Clint?

Sheriff Moreland had recommended Barkley to Clint, recommended Vance Restin's lawyer to fight the charges Vance Restin had brought against him. Terry had been right not to trust Moreland.

Clint left Buck, told him that Eclipse was behind the Drinkwater.

"I'll look after him," Buck said. "Do what you gotta do, Adams."

"Thanks."

He left the saloon and walked to the lawyer's office, hoping to find him there.

He entered the office without knocking and the young lawyer looked up from his desk.

"Why do I have a feeling this visit is not good news?" Barkley asked.

"You're Vance Restin's lawyer."

"You're not supposed to know that," Barkley said.

"But now that I do..."

"What do you want?"

"I need to see a copy of Terry Restin's mother's will."

"That old thing?" Barkley asked. "I don't even think I can find a copy—"

"I know," Clint said, "you keep a messy office, but I

have a feeling you know exactly where it is."

Now Barkley frowned.

"If I show you that, I could lose my biggest client."

"If you don't show it to me," Clint told him, "you could lose a lot more."

"Is that a threat, Mr. Adams?"

"It certainly is, Mr. Barkley."

"Can I ask why you want to see it?"

"Vance Restin sent four gunmen to kill me and his daughter," Clint said. "I have a feeling that will has the answer to why."

"Kill his own daughter?" Barkley said. "Well, that's—that's just ridiculous."

"Nevertheless, I need to see that will," Clint said, "now!"

Barkley looked past Clint at the door to the office.

"No one's coming to help you, Eugene," Clint said, "and you'll never make it past me to the door."

Barkley took a deep breath and let it out slowly.

"Well," he said, finally, "I suppose if Restin really did try to have his daughter killed, we should know why."

"You don't already know?"

"I'll find that will."

*****

Barkley sat quietly behind his desk while Clint read Terry's mother's will.

"There was a lot of money in her family," Clint said.

"Yes," the lawyer said.

"And her father controls it...until she's twenty one."

"Right again."

Clint lowered the will and stared at the lawyer.

"I know what you're thinking," Barkley said.

"And what are you thinking?" Clint said.

Barkley sighed and said, "I'm thinking I may be losing my best client."

"I just can't believe a man would have his own daughter killed, even for millions of dollars."

"You don't know how much Vance Restin needs that money," Barkley said.

"Needs it? You mean he's broke?"

"No," Barkley said, "I just mean he needs to have money...needs to be rich."

"Needs it enough to kill his own daughter."

Barley spread his arms and said, "You tell me."

Clint put the will down on the young man's desk and stood up.

"You better tell me right now how loyal you are to Restin, Eugene," he said.

"Well, he's a client—but so are you."

"Oh yeah," Clint said. "I'm a client all of you were planning to keep in jail if I didn't take Restin's job."

"All of us?"

"You, Restin, the sheriff."

"You think we were all working together—"

"No," Clint said, "I think you and Moreland were working for Restin...period."

"Mr. Adams—"

"Eugene," Clint said, "you need to stay in your office. I don't want you to tell Restin I was here."

"Are you asking me, or..."

"I'm telling," Clint said. "And I won't take it kindly if you cross me."

Nervously, the young lawyer said, "So you're... threatening me?"

"If that's what it takes," Clint said, "let's say I'm threatening you."

171

FORTY-THREE

Clint decided not to stop in and see the sheriff. He certainly couldn't trust that Moreland would not go right to Restin and tell him that he was back. The lawman wouldn't scare as much as the lawyer did.

He stopped into a small café for some food, wrapped it up, and took it back to the Drinkwater with him.

"How did it go?" Buck asked. The front door was open again. Clint didn't bother telling him to lock it this time.

"Just like I thought," Clint said. "She's supposed to get her mother's money when she turns twenty one, which she recently did."

"You'd think he would've killed her before that," Buck said.

"That's what I thought," Clint said. "His lawyer's been holding up the transfer as long as he can. I think it took a while for Restin to finally make his decision."

"So what are you gonna do?"

"I'm going to talk to Terry and see what she wants to do," Clint said. "After all, the money's hers."

"Well, whatever happens," Buck said, "I'm with you. I'd kinda like to get my place back."

"We'll work on that, Buck," Clint promised.

*****

He rode back out to the small house and found, to his relief, that Terry had listened to him and stayed put.

"What'd you bring?" she asked anxiously.

"Fried chicken."

"Ooh," she said, "gimme."

He handed her the wrapped package and she tore into it and started on a chicken leg.

"What about you?" she asked.

"Give me a wing."

She passed it over to him and they sat on the floor and ate.

"What did you find out?"

She listened intently as he explained everything he'd learned from Buck, and then from Eugene Barkley after reading the will.

When he was done she sat there, chewing, looking slightly stunned.

"I never knew," she said. "I never knew my mother left the money to me."

"Your father didn't want you to know," he said. "That much is obvious."

"Oh my God," she said, "he really does want me dead, doesn't he?"

He reached out and touched her hand. This was obviously the moment that fact had become very real for her.

"What do I do?" she asked.

"We'll have to make sure," he said, "he never gets the chance to do it again."

"You mean...kill him first? Oh Clint, I may not love him, but I don't think I can--"

"No," Clint said, "not that. We have to prove he tried to have you killed."

"You mean...legally?"

"Yes," he said.

"And send him to jail?"

"Can you do that?"

She firmed her jaw and said, "Oh yes, I can do that. I can do that for my mother."

"Well," Clint said, "why don't we do it for your mother, and do it for you, too while we're at it?"

He grabbed a chicken leg and, in the absence of glasses, they clinked legs as she said, "Agreed."

FORTY-FOUR

Vance Restin came out onto his front porch, wearing a gun on his hip. Two men turned to face him. Both wore guns on their own hips in worn holsters. Restin preferred to employ men whose guns looked used rather than men with new guns and pristine leather holsters.

"You're two of the new men?"

"Yessir."

"What are your names?"

"Heath," one of them said, "and this is Stiller."

"You men know how to use those guns?"

"We do, sir," Stiller said. Both men were in their late thirties with several days of stubble on their faces.

"You've killed men before?"

The two men exchanged a glance and then Heath said, "That's pretty much our job."

"You've heard of the Gunsmith?"

"We sure have."

"Not afraid to go up against him?"

"Lookin' forward to it," Heath said.

"Either of you ever seen him before?"

"I have," Heath said.

"Good," Restin said, "then you'll recognize him." He turned to go back inside, then stopped and turned back. "He won't know you, will he?"

"Naw," Heath said, "he never heard of us."

177

"That's good. What about the other new men?"

"Everybody knows how to shoot, Mr. Restin," Heath said.

"And the more you pay," Stiller said with a grin, "the better we shoot."

"I'll keep that in mind," Restin said.

"Mr. Restin," Heath said, as the rancher started for the door again.

"Yes?"

"If you don't mind me sayin' so," the man said, "Adams will never come here."

"Why not?"

"He's no fool," Heath said. "You have too many men."

"You're all here to keep me alive."

"Yeah, but we could do that by killin' him," Stiller said. "And we can't kill him if he don't come here."

"What do you suggest?"

"We think we should go and find him," Heath said, "track him down."

"Where would you start?"

"In town."

"Why would he go to town?" Restin asked.

"Because," Heath said, "he wouldn't come here."

Restin turned to squarely face the men.

"Why do I think you men weren't out here on the porch by accident?"

"We weren't," Heath said. "We were waitin' for you."

"Why?"

"Stiller and I are the best guns you've got," Heath said. "Keep the others here and let us go and find Adams."

"We'll kill him for you," Stiller said.

"Just the two of you?"

"We have some other...friends," Heath said.

178

"I sent four men after him," Restin said, "and they never came back."

"We're six," Stiller said, "and we're better than they were."

Restin thought a moment.

"If you men kill Adams," he said, "I'll triple what you were promised."

"Not a problem, Mr. Restin," Heath said, 'but before we go we'll needed a little more information from you."

"Whatever you need," Restin said, "just ask."

FORTY-FIVE

"Keep that fire low," Clint told Terry. "We don't want the light to be seen."

"I told you," she said, "my father would never come here."

"Just to be on the safe side."

"Why don't we cover the windows?" she asked.

"With what?"

"Good point."

They had eaten and finished the coffee. The only reason to keep the fire at all was a little warmth.

"Why don't we just put it out and depend on the blankets?" she suggested.

"Would you be warm enough?"

She smiled and said, "If we were sharing the same blanket, yes."

"Well," he said, "that is an idea."

He stomped out the fire, and then they wrapped themselves together in one blanket.

When she started moving her hands around beneath the blanket he said, "Behave yourself."

"Why?"

"Because this isn't the time or the place," he said. "Besides, you're too young."

"That didn't seem to bother you on the trail."

"I didn't know how young you were then."

"I'm twenty one, Clint," she said. "I'm a woman." She kissed his neck, slid her hand inside his shirt.

"Terry..."

"Come on, Clint," she said, her breath hot in his ear. "What else do we have to do?"

She undid the buttons on her shirt and pulled his hand inside. He found her nipple, squeezed it with his thumb and forefinger. She caught her breath.

She was right. What else did they have to do?

He kissed her, her mouth eager, her tongue active, her hands undoing his shirt and his belt. He slipped off his gun belt, set it on the floor close by.

They unwrapped themselves from the blanket, instead spread it on the floor, then undressed each other.

"Wait," she said, when he reached for her. She got on her hands and knees, presented her smooth butt to him and said, "Like this."

"Oh," he said, "you're a bad girl."

"I've heard about it," she said, "but I've never done it. I want to do it with you."

"For this you need to be wet," he said, reaching between her thighs. She was wet, but as he slid his fingers into her vagina, she became even more so. He wet his fingers thoroughly, causing her to gasp, then spread the cheek of her ass and wet her anus as much as he could. When he slid his middle finger into her she tensed.

"You have to relax," he said. "You have to be very relaxed."

"I—I can't," she said.

"You said you wanted it."

"I do," she said. "I don't mean—what I mean is, I'm too excited to relax."

He used his hand on her again, getting it wet and slick from her pussy, then applying it to her tender butthole.

"Try," he said.

He positioned himself behind her, pressed the head of his cock to her slick anus, and pushed slowly.

"Oh," she said, "oh...oh...yesssss..."

*****

Later she snuggled up against him for more warmth. "Do you have a plan yet?"

"Your father will have his ranch too well guarded," Clint said. "We've got to get him away from there."

"How?"

He closed his eyes and said, "I'll think about that tomorrow."

*****

Dexter Heath and Pete Stiller collected four more of their compadres and rode out the next morning. Armed with information from Vance Restin—possibly information he, himself, didn't know he had—Heath had an idea where they might find Clint Adams and the girl.

"You want Adams dead," Heath had said that morning before riding out. "And the girl?"

"There's a bonus if you get both of them."

Restin was a cold one, paying to have his own daughter killed, but that didn't concern Heath very much.

"What makes you think they're gonna be out here?" Ron Finn asked.

"Something the old man said," Heath replied. "About a house the girl was born in." If Adams wanted to hide out, and stay away from town, he'd need help, since he didn't know the area. The girl, on the other hand, did.

"And if they ain't there?"

"I'll deal with that if it happens," Heath said. "We

know the Gunsmith can't stay hidden in town. I bet the girl takes him to this house."

"Sounds good to me," Stiller said.

Finn shrugged, and the other three men looked unconcerned. They were getting paid, that's all they cared about.

*****

Clint woke to the sound of horses.

"Terry!" he said. "Wake up!"

"What is it?" She took her head off his shoulder, looked up at him.

"Get up!" he said. "Riders."

They both got to their feet. Clint grabbed his rifle and held it out to the girl.

"Take this!"

"Clint—how'd they find us?"

"Somebody got smart," he said, "that's all. Take that window."

They each went to a window on either side of the front door. Clint looked out in time to see six well armed riders appear.

"Oh God," she said, "there's six of them."

"Yeah," he said, "more gunmen hired by your father."

"Clint, I'm so sorry," she said. "Hiding here wasn't such a good idea, after all."

"It's not your fault," he said. "I'm sure you were right about your father. He wouldn't come here, but one of these men figured it out."

"Do you know them?"

"I know every one of them," he said, "without knowing any of their names."

"Maybe they won't know we're here," she said, her

tone hopeful.

"The horses are out back," he said. "They know." He should have brought the horses inside, but it was too late for recriminations.

"What do we do?" she asked. "Do we shoot?"

"No," Clint said, "we have to let them make the first move. That means we just wait."

FORTY-SIX

Heath had one of his men, Lincoln, go around back. When he returned he said, "Two horses, one a big Arabian."

"That's the Gunsmith's horse."

"Want me to shoot it?"

Heath glared at Lincoln.

"No, I don't want you to shoot the horse! Is there a back door?"

"No."

"Windows?"

"Yes."

"Then take Harris and cover the back. Do not shoot that horse, do you understand?"

"Sure, Heath, sure."

"Go!"

*****

Clint saw two of the men split off from the rest, undoubtedly, to cover the back.

"Clint? What's that mean?"

"It means they've got the front and back covered." He looked around. There were no side windows.

"We're trapped!" Terry said.

"Take it easy," he said.

"How can you say that?"

"Because the perfect way to get killed is to panic," he told her. "Who has more experience in these situations, Terry, me or you?"

"You, but—"

"So take a deep breath and relax," Clint said. "I'm going to talk to whoever's out there and find out just how bad a situation we really are in. Okay?"

"Okay."

But before Clint could put his plan into practice, a voice from outside called, "Adams! Clint Adams!"

*****

"What are we gonna do?" Stiller asked Heath. "By now he knows we're here."

"That's fine," Heath said. "Let's see if we can get the Gunsmith to come outside and go out in a blaze of glory." He turned away from Stiller and called out, "Adams! Clint Adams!"

*****

"This is Clint Adams!" Clint called back. "Who am I talking to?"

"It doesn't really matter," the man called out. "You don't know me, but my name is Heath."

"You're right," Clint said. "I don't know you."

"Doesn't matter," Heath said. "All you need to know is that there are six of us, and we're here for you...and the girl."

"Who hired you?" Clint asked. "Her father?"

"That doesn't matter," Heath said. "What matters is you're in a bad situation. You can't get out of there unless we let you out."

"And why would you do that?"

"So you can face us and go out like a man," Heath called. "Or, like a legend."

"You can't go out there," Terry said to him.

"Shh," he said. "Heath, what about the girl?"

"What about her?" Heath asked. "If you face us and win, she comes out alive."

"And if you kill me?"

"Sorry," Heath said, "but she's part of the job."

"Give me a minute to think about it."

"That's what you've got," Heath said, "sixty seconds."

Clint ducked down beneath the window, his back against the wall.

"You can't really be considering this?" Terry said.

"What else can we do?"

"But...have you ever faced six men before?"

"Yes."

"And?"

"It didn't end well."

"But...you're still alive."

"Just barely, after that."

He skittered across the floor to his saddlebags, took out the Colt new Line.

"Even with two guns..." she said.

"Terry, we can shoot it out with them, but eventually they'll come in. We'll run out of ammo before they do or this house will fall down around our ears."

"Maybe," she said, "maybe help will come."

"From where?"

"I—I...don't know."

"Neither do I," Clint said. "Look, you have to stay inside."

"I can help."

"If things go bad out there, I'll need your help," he said. "If I go down you just start shooting."

"B-but, if they kill you..."

"I'm going to do my best to make sure they don't," he said. He knew if they killed him, she wouldn't live much longer.

"Clint—"

"Just be ready to shoot," he told her, and looked out the window again.

FORTY-SEVEN

"Do you think he'll come out?" Stiller asked.

"What choice does he have?" Heath said. "He'd rather go out standing on his feet than crouching down in that shack."

"If we gun him down out in the open," Stiller said, "it's gonna be a big deal."

"A very big deal, my friend," Heath said. "Very big."

*****

"Heath!" Clint yelled.

"Five seconds to spare, Adams."

"I have a condition."

"What's that?"

"I'm going to kill five of you," Clint called, "and keep one of you alive."

Heath chuckled. "And why's that?"

"Because that last man is going to tell me who you're all working for," Clint said. "If he does that, I'll let him live and walk away."

"That's up to you, Adams," Heath said. "If you live, you can do whatever you want."

"I just want your other men to know that."

"They know it!"

"Then I'm coming out."

*****

The other two men with Heath and Stiller—Haywood and Cassidy—looked at each other, and then at Heath.

"Is he serious?" Haywood asked.

"He's managed to stay alive this long," Heath said. "I'd say he's always serious."

The door to the house opened.

*****

Clint opened the door and stepped out.

Four men were standing in front of him, and from either side of the house came the fifth and sixth man. They were all within his sight, which he found odd. If he was on the other side he would have stretched them out so that he'd have to turn his head to see them all. He could make out the fifth and sixth man from the corners of his eyes.

Of the men standing ahead of him, he was able to pick out the man called Heath.

"You're Heath," he said, looking directly at the man.

"That's right," Heath said. "How could you tell?"

"You look like you're in charge."

"I'll take that as a compliment."

"Don't," Clint said. "I'm going to kill you first."

The other men shifted their feet nervously. Clint knew he was seeming way too confident to suit them. That was his goal. Nerve would make them rush their shots. That was his only chance to survive.

"I suppose you'll want—" Heath started to say, but Clint didn't give him time to finish. Talking too much was another way to get killed. When it came to this kind of a situation, the only thing that helped was getting it done.

He drew both guns, the modified Colt from his holster and the New Line from his belt.

*****

Terry watched in awe from the window, her rifle ready if Clint needed her. She could see Clint and all six men he was facing.

As promised, he killed the man called Heath first, shooting him right in the center if the chest. The other men were all clawing for their guns as he turned both guns on them. He extended both hands out from his sides and shot the fifth and sixth men, who had come around from behind the house.

The other three men seemed to be pulling their triggers even before they brought their guns up. Two of them actually fired their guns into the ground.

Clint stood stock still, brought both guns to bear on the remaining three men. He shot two of them, one with each gun, even as the sixth man managed to fire a shot at him that missed cleanly.

With five men on the ground, Clint pointed both guns at the last man standing...

"What's your name?" he asked.

"Finn," the man said. He had his gun in his hand, but firing it again seemed to be the last thing on his mind.

"You're the last man."

"Yessir."

"You heard what I said to Heath about the last man?" Clint asked.

"Yessir, I did."

"Then drop your gun."

Finn obeyed. His gun hit the ground.

"Now I need to know who you and your friends were

working for.''

"N-no problem, Mr. Adams," Finn said. "Vance Restin.''

"Restin sent you to kill me?''

"Yessir.''

"And his daughter?''

Clint heard the door to the house open and Terry stepped out, holding the rifle down. She wanted to hear the answer to this.

"He s-said—he promised if we killed you both, there'd be a big bonus.''

"Okay, Finn," Clint said, "I'm going to need you to tell that to the sheriff, and then you can go.''

"The s-sheriff?'' Finn repeated. "He ain't gonna let me go.''

"I guarantee he will," Clint said. "All you have to do is ride back to town with me.''

"O-okay.''

"But first we have to tie your partners to their saddles," Clint added. "We'll be taking them in, too.''

"S-sure." Finn still seemed unsure as to whether or not Clint was going to kill him.

"Relax," Clint said. He slid the New Line into his belt, then replaced the spent rounds in his Colt with live ones before holstering it. "I need you alive.''

"Y-yessir.''

"Start dragging your partners over.''

"Y-yessir.''

While Finn did that, Terry turned to Clint and asked, "You really think the sheriff is going to arrest my father?''

"Does a circuit judge really come to town?" Clint asked her.

"Yes, he does.''

"The sheriff may work for your father, but not the

circuit judge," Clint said. "The sheriff's not going to have much of a choice. He'll bring your father in, but it's the judge who will file the charges."

"I hope you're right."

"I am right," Clint said, "and you're going to be a very rich girl."

FORTY-EIGHT

Sheriff Moreland made the arrest.

"You're going to pay for this, Moreland," Restin told him from a cell. "I'll have your job."

"You're probably right," Moreland said. "I could look the other way on a lot of things, Restin, but having your own daughter killed? That ain't one of them."

He left Restin still sputtering in his cell, left the cellblock, and closed the door.

*****

Clint had to stay in town and wait for the circuit judge to arrive, as did the gunman Finn. Moreland agreed not to lock Finn up. It was that or leave and have the Gunsmith tracking him down.

When the judge arrived, he wasted no time charging Restin once he heard the evidence. There was no need for Clint to stay for the trial, but there was one other thing he had to see to.

*****

Clint took Terry to the office of Eugene Barkley, Attorney at Law.

"This is your lawyer now," he told her.

The young lawyer smiled from behind his desk and

197

said, "Miss Restin."

"B-but, aren't you representing my father?"

"Not anymore," Barkley said. "He'll have to get someone else to defend him against criminal charges. Meanwhile, you need to sign a few papers, and then you'll be a very rich young lady."

She looked at Clint, who nodded and held a chair for her to sit in.

*****

When they stepped outside, Terry Restin was very rich.

"What do I do now?" she asked.

"You can run your father's businesses or sell them," Clint said.

"I don't know the first thing about business."

"Then you better sell his holdings. Barkley will help you with that."

"B-but, what about the ranch?"

"You can keep living there."

"I guess—I could keep Ray on as foreman."

"Do you trust him?"

"He only worked for my father," she said. "I know he didn't approve of a lot of what he did."

"And what about the Drinkwater?"

"I'll give that back to Buck."

"See?" Clint said. "You're already making the right decisions."

ABOUT THE AUTHOR

As "J.R. Roberts" Bob Randisi is the creator and author of the long running western series, *The Gunsmith*. Under various other pseudonyms he has created and written the "Tracker," "Mountain Jack Pike," "Angel Eyes," "Ryder," "Talbot Roper," "The Son of Daniel Shaye," and "the Gamblers" Western series. His western short story collection, *The Cast-Iron Star and Other Western Stories*, is now available in print and as an ebook from Western Fictioneers Books.

In the mystery genre he is the author of the *Miles Jacoby, Nick Delvecchio, Gil & Claire Hunt, Dennis McQueen, Joe Keough,* and *The Rat Pack,* series. He has written more than 500 western novels and has worked in the Western, Mystery, Sci-Fi, Horror and Spy genres. He is the editor of over 30 anthologies. All told he is the author of over 650 novels. His arms are very, very tired.

He is the founder of the Private Eye Writers of America, the creator of the Shamus Award, the co-founder of Mystery Scene Magazine, the American Crime Writers League, Western Fictioneers and their Peacemaker Award.

In 2009 the Private Eye Writers of America awarded him the Life Achievement Award, and in 2013 the Readwest Foundation presented him with their President's Award for Life Achievement.

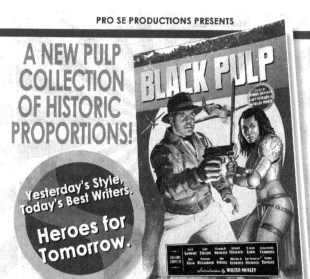

Made in the USA
Lexington, KY
26 January 2017